GANGED UP

Longarm hooked a short punch to Kelly's midsection. His fist traveled about six inches, but it landed with such force that it was buried almost to the wrist in the man's belly. Kelly's florid face turned pale as he gasped in surprise and pain.

"I warned you, old son," Longarm muttered.

Kelly stumbled back a step, clutching himself. His mouth opened and closed as he tried unsuccessfully to form words. The men with him moved forward, as surprised as Kelly himself to see their leader stricken helpless like that. But they were angry too, and when Kelly finally got his voice back and choked out, "Get the bastard!" they lunged at Longarm with fists swinging . . .

TABOR EVANS

LONGARM

AND THE
SCARLET RIDER

JOVE BOOKS, NEW YORK

THE BERKLEY PUBLISHING GROUP
Published by the Penguin Group
Penguin Group (USA) Inc.
375 Hudson Street, New York, New York 10014, USA
Penguin Group (Canada), 90 Eglinton Avenue East, Suite 700, Toronto, Ontario M4P 2Y3, Canada
(a division of Pearson Penguin Canada Inc.)
Penguin Books Ltd., 80 Strand, London WC2R 0RL, England
Penguin Group Ireland, 25 St. Stephen's Green, Dublin 2, Ireland (a division of Penguin Books Ltd.)
Penguin Group (Australia), 250 Camberwell Road, Camberwell, Victoria 3124, Australia
(a division of Pearson Australia Group Pty. Ltd.)
Penguin Books India Pvt. Ltd., 11 Community Centre, Panchsheel Park, New Delhi—110 017, India
Penguin Group (NZ), Cnr. Airborne and Rosedale Roads, Albany, Auckland 1310, New Zealand
(a division of Pearson New Zealand Ltd.)
Penguin Books (South Africa) (Pty.) Ltd., 24 Sturdee Avenue, Rosebank, Johannesburg 2196,
South Africa

Penguin Books Ltd., Registered Offices: 80 Strand, London WC2R 0RL, England

LONGARM AND THE SCARLET RIDER

A Jove Book / published by arrangement with the author

PRINTING HISTORY
Jove edition / October 2005

ISBN: 0-515-14019-8

JOVE®
Jove Books are published by The Berkley Publishing Group,
a division of Penguin Group (USA) Inc.,
375 Hudson Street, New York, New York 10014.
JOVE is a registered trademark of Penguin Group (USA) Inc.
The "J" design is a trademark belonging to Penguin Group (USA) Inc.

PRINTED IN THE UNITED STATES OF AMERICA

10 9 8 7 6 5 4 3 2 1

Chapter 1

To Longarm's way of thinking, the barrel of the old Dragoon Colt pointed at his head looked about as big around as the mouth of a cannon. About as dangerous too.

"Take it easy, old son," he said as calmly as possible. "I ain't trying to steal your squaw."

The gun trembled a little in the hand of the white-bearded, buckskin-clad old man who held it, but not enough to give Longarm any hope that he was about to drop the massive revolver.

"How the hell can you say that when I come in here and find her sittin' on your lap big as you please, mister? No, there ain't no two ways about it. I got to kill you. Little Fawn too maybe. I'll have to think on that."

Little Fawn savvied enough white-man talk to know what the old-timer had said. She shuddered in fear, which made her plump, toothsome rump wiggle around a good deal where she had plopped it down on Longarm's groin. That didn't help the situation any because the wiggling made his pecker start to get hard, and Little Fawn squirmed even more when she felt it poking against her.

This was a hell of a mess, thought Longarm, and it wasn't even his fault.

He hadn't come into this prairie roadhouse looking for female companionship. He'd been after a drink and a little information, namely whether or not he was still in the United States or if he had crossed the border into Canada. Out here on the vast, windswept plains, it was a mite difficult to keep up with things like international boundary lines. At least down along the Rio Grande, a gent knew whether he was in Texas or Mexico, depending on which side of the river he was on.

Longarm had gotten the drink from a little old bald-headed man who reminded him of his boss down in Denver, Chief Marshal Billy Vail. He had even found out that he was in Canada, as he suspected. But when he sat down at a table to take a load off for a spell, this pleasantly rounded, pretty Indian gal had come in, spotted him, and made a beeline for his lap. He had no doubt she wanted to take him to her lodge, where she would invite him into her buffalo robes in exchange for a coin or two. Longarm might have considered it had he not been working, but before he even had time to ponder the question, that Dragoon-toting Methuselah in buckskins had come in and thrown down on him.

That would be a hell of a way to die, brains blown out over a gal he didn't even want.

He tried one more time to be reasonable. "Listen to me. I just met Little Fawn here. I didn't invite her to sit on my lap." She gave him a hurt look over her shoulder. Longarm forged ahead. "She's every bit as pretty as her name, but I wouldn't steal her from you, old son. It just wouldn't be an honorable thing to do."

The bald-headed proprietor of the roadhouse spoke up nervously, not wanting his place shot up. "The stranger's tellin' the truth, Dooley. He was just sittin' there when Little Fawn came in and jumped on him."

The barrel of the Dragoon drooped a little as the old-timer frowned. "You mean he didn't offer her money or whiskey or candy?"

The proprietor shook his head. "Not a blessed thing. In fact, he looked mighty surprised when she sat down on his lap and made herself right at home."

Longarm was glad the hombre had spoken up. Other than him, the roadhouse was empty, with no other customers to take Longarm's side in this matter.

"Well, all right then." The old-timer finally pointed the big pistol at the puncheon floor and carefully lowered the hammer. "I reckon I won't have to kill him. Or her. Little Fawn really ought to get a beatin' for actin' so brazen, though."

Little Fawn sniffed and stood up. Longarm got the feeling that since she probably outweighed the skinny old man by a considerable amount, there wouldn't be any beatings handed out. She sashayed over to the bar and pointedly ignored the old-timer.

With a disgusted snort, the old man holstered the Dragoon, which was damned near as big as he was, and came over to the table. He stuck out a gnarled paw.

"Sorry I misjudged you, mister. I can tell now that you're a gentleman."

Longarm shook his hand and said, "Sorry for the misunderstanding." He was glad that the table concealed his crotch. The stiffness in his shaft was taking its time going away, and it might have been awkward if the old man had seen it poking up against the front of his jeans. "Dooley, is it?"

"Dooley McCarren."

Longarm waved a hand at the table. "Sit down and have a drink with me."

"Don't mind if I do." Dooley grinned, though it was hard to see the expression in the thick, white beard. He sat down on the other side of the rough-hewn table and motioned for the bartender to bring him a drink.

"Doing some trapping?" Longarm asked.

"Yeah. It ain't like it was thirty, forty years ago when I first come out here. Too many of the beaver and the other critters are gone now. But I still get a few plews whenever I go up into the mountains."

The Rockies—the Canadian Rockies, Longarm reminded himself—were about a hundred miles west of here. It was the middle of summer, past the prime trapping season. Dooley would probably go back to the mountains for a while during the fall, take a few more pelts, and then find a place to spend the winter. With Little Fawn and her people, more than likely. After decades out here, a lot of the old trappers were more Indian than white.

The proprietor brought over a drink and said, "Here you go, Dooley."

"Thanks, Ashford." Dooley tossed back the whiskey, then licked the few drops that had caught in his mustache. He looked at Longarm. "What's your handle, mister?"

"Custis Parker." That was a stretch, since Parker was really his middle name, but he wasn't going to introduce himself as Deputy United States Marshal Custis Long, which he would have had to do if he was being totally honest. For one thing, when he was working he made a habit of not announcing that he was a lawman until he had to, and for another, he was out of his jurisdiction up here. He knew that and didn't much give a damn.

"Pleased to meet you, Parker. Cowboy, ain't you?"

Truth to tell, Longarm *had* done some cowboying in his time, years earlier when he had first come west after the Late Unpleasantness between North and South. He hadn't wrangled bovines for a living for quite some time, though. But in his garb of jeans, butternut shirt, denim jacket, and flat-crowned, snuff-brown Stetson, he could easily pass for a drifting cowpoke. At the moment, that was exactly his intention, so he nodded in answer to Dooley McCarren's question.

4

"That's right. You wouldn't know of any riding jobs around here, would you?"

Dooley made a face and spat on the floor. Behind the bar, bald-headed Ashford rolled his eyes.

"I ain't that fond of cow nurses," Dooley said. "In your case, I'll make an exception, Parker, because you seem like a pretty good fella. But I don't have any truck with the ranchers and wouldn't know who was hirin' and who ain't."

Longarm nodded. "I understand. Appreciate you being honest with me."

"I ain't got nothin' against 'em personally, you understand. It's just that I recollect when these plains were covered by buffalo durin' the summer. A magnificent sight it was too. Now the buffs are mostly gone, and the cattlemen are movin' in. Right now it's still open range, but the time will come . . ." Dooley shook his head sadly. "The time will come when they'll put up fences and finish the job o' ruinin' this country for the folks who first came out here."

"You had to know when they started building the railroad across the country to the Pacific that the cattlemen would follow it."

Dooley smacked a calloused palm on the table. "Waugh! Don't get me started on that damn iron horse! A-smokin' and a-bellerin' and a-stinkin' up the plains—" He broke off and shook his head. "No, don't get me started. Just thinkin' about it angrifies my blood too much."

"Yeah, it's a hellacious thing." Longarm casually ignored Dooley's admonition to drop the subject and continued. "I saw it with my own eyes down in the States. Some folks call the railhead Hell on Wheels, because whenever it picks up and moves, it brings all sorts of wickedness with it. Gamblers and whiskey peddlers and whores. *Lots* of whores."

Dooley shook his head. "A pox on all of 'em."

"How far is the railhead from here?"

5

Dooley didn't answer, but Ashford had heard the question from behind the bar and said, "About five miles north of here, mister. You thinkin' about goin' up there?"

"I might."

"Perdition and purgatory," Dooley muttered in his beard. "That's all you'll find there."

Longarm shrugged. "Sometimes a fella's got to see the elephant for himself."

"You're a bigger fool than I thought then." Dooley stood up. "Come on, Little Fawn."

At the bar, Little Fawn ignored him.

In frustration, Dooley blew his breath out through his drooping mustache and walked over to her to take her arm. "Come on."

She turned and leaned over to whisper in his ear.

Dooley nodded. "Yeah, I'll do that to you, if that's what you want. You got to take it a mite easier on me, though. These old bones o' mine ain't as limber as they used to be."

Little Fawn laughed and rubbed her hand on Dooley's arm. Together they walked out of the roadhouse, but on the way out the door Little Fawn cast one last lascivious glance over her shoulder at Longarm. Then they were gone.

Better Dooley than him thought Longarm, as he drank the last of the whiskey in his glass. He stood up and carried the empty over to the bar.

"Are you really ridin' up to end-of-track, mister?" Ashford asked.

Longarm nodded. "I reckon so."

Ashford sighed. "When the railroad's finished, that'll be the end of this place. I don't do hardly enough business now to keep me in provisions. Nobody'll ride the old trails anymore once they can sit back in luxury inside a railcar and zoom along at damn near a mile a minute."

"There are bound to be some old-timers like Dooley who don't like the railroad."

Ashford gave a snort. "Dooley don't spend any money.

Anything he makes on his pelts, he sends it back down to somebody in the States. A wife probably."

"Little Fawn's not his wife?" It was a deliberately naïve, question.

"Little Fawn's his squaw. An old man like Dooley's probably had half a dozen squaws sharin' his blankets over the years, maybe more."

Longarm rubbed his jaw. "These whores up at the railhead . . . Who would a fella talk to about meeting up with some of them?"

"Damned if I know. Just walk down the street. You'll probably trip over two or three of 'em a-lyin' back just waitin' for some gent to climb on."

Longarm nodded. "Much obliged." He took a couple of coins from his pocket and slid them across the bar. "That's for Dooley's drink."

The money disappeared, and Ashford nodded. "Thanks, mister."

Longarm walked out of the roadhouse. A couple of trails crossed here, which was likely the reason Ashford had chosen the location for his business in the first place. But the sod building was the only sign of habitation for miles around except for a few tipis poking up in the distance. Probably Little Fawn's people, thought Longarm. Business was bad, all right.

So Longarm untied the reins of the chestnut gelding he had borrowed from a U.S. Army fort across the line, swung up into the saddle, and rode north toward the railhead and the Canadian version of Hell on Wheels.

Chapter 2

A week earlier, Longarm had sat in Billy Vail's office in the Federal Building in Denver and listened as the chief marshal said, "I know you've been to Canada before, Custis. Have any hankering to go back?"

Longarm thought about the cases that had taken him north of the border. "Not particularly, Billy. I got shot at up there."

Vail snorted. "You get shot at everywhere you go."

Longarm nodded solemnly. "It does seem like it, don't it?"

"Anyway, I got a job here that needs a man to go up to the northern part of Montana." Vail shoved some papers across the desk. "Could be that whoever takes it might wind up having to cross the line."

Longarm picked up the reports but didn't look at them yet. "A U.S. deputy marshal don't have any authority up in Canada. You ought to know that better than anybody, Billy, seeing as you're chief marshal."

Vail's mostly bald scalp flushed pink. He looked like a cherub, sitting behind his desk like that, all pudgy and soft. But Longarm knew that Vail wasn't anywhere near as soft as he looked. In his earlier years, Vail had packed a badge for the Texas Rangers, and he'd had a well-deserved reputation as a hell-roaring lawman.

For the moment, though, Vail kept a tight rein on his temper. "I know you'd be out of your jurisdiction, Custis. That's why I plan to send a wire to the commissioner of the Mounties, asking for their cooperation."

"The Mounties, eh?" Longarm had worked with the North West Mounted Police before, and knew them to be efficient lawmen most of the time. Some of them were a mite too fond of consuming the goods they confiscated from whiskey smugglers, and they could be stiff-necked hombres with all that Queen and Country business, but all in all Longarm didn't have any problem with the Mounties.

"That's right. You won't be going it alone for a change, if you have to cross over into Canada." Vail poked a finger at the documents in Longarm's hand. "Now read those reports. Henry went to all the trouble to type up extra copies, so you might as well take them with you."

"I ain't said I wanted the job yet, Billy."

Vail snorted. "Read the reports."

Longarm scanned the words that had been typed by Vail's four-eyed secretary, and as their meaning soaked in on his brain, he looked across the desk at his boss.

"This sounds bad, Billy. Mighty bad."

"A dozen girls and young women gone missing in two months' time . . ." Vail nodded. "Yeah, I'd say that's bad, all right."

The reports came from several settlements in the northern reaches of Montana, not far from the Canadian border. The missing women, ranging in ages from sixteen to twenty-five, came from a variety of backgrounds. Some were the daughters of Army officers posted to Fort Shaw or Fort Assiniboine; one was the wife of a lieutenant. There were a couple of schoolteachers in the bunch, a seamstress, a cook, even a missionary. Other than being fairly young, they seemed to have little in common.

Longarm tapped the reports. "I ain't saying it's the case here, but now and then a gal has been known to up and disappear on her own. Say she's sweet on a fella but her daddy won't allow her to see the young gent. Or she's married but meets somebody she likes better than her husband."

Vail nodded. "Sure, it's been known to happen. But in every one of these cases, the people who reported the missing women claimed that everything was fine, that they didn't have any reason to run off."

"Well, of course that's what they'd say." Longarm sounded skeptical.

"Listen, Custis, that's why we're investigating. The fact that some of those gals come from Army families is enough to bring the Justice Department in on it. Also, the governor of Montana Territory asked for our help, since the disappearances stretch over several counties up there. If you find that some of them ran off on their own . . . well, we're not in the business of rounding up stray females. But if they were taken against their will . . ."

"I'll get to the bottom of it, Billy. You can count on that."

Vail looked more like a cherub than ever as a smile spread across his round face. "I knew you'd say that, Custis. That's why I had Henry type up those extra copies of the reports and get you some train tickets."

Longarm just grunted. Billy Vail knew him pretty well by now. He ought to, as many years as the two of them had worked together.

Henry knew him pretty well too, as Longarm discovered when he stopped in the outer office to pick up his train tickets and expense vouchers. The young fella pushed them across the desk and smirked.

"Going to Canada, I hear."

"Maybe. Don't really know yet."

"I have a telegram here to send to the commissioner of the North West Mounted Police. You'll be under his command if you cross the border."

11

Longarm frowned. Vail had said he was going to request the Mounties' cooperation. He hadn't mentioned anything about Longarm having to take orders from them. He started to turn back to the door.

Henry's smug voice stopped him. "That bothers you, doesn't it? The idea of taking orders."

"I ain't overly fond of it."

"I warned Marshal Vail you'd cause trouble about that part of the assignment."

Longarm's eyes narrowed. "You did, did you?"

"That's right. You have enough trouble just taking orders from Marshal Vail."

Longarm took a cheroot out of his vest pocket, put it in his mouth, and clamped his teeth down on it, leaving it unlit. "We'll just see about that." Instead of going back into the inner office, he stuffed all the paperwork in his pocket and stalked out.

He was halfway back to his rented room on the other side of Cherry Creek to gather his traveling gear before he realized that Henry had played him like a fiddle, getting his dander up but then skillfully getting him out of the office before he could bitch at Vail. Longarm stopped on the street, shook his head, and chuckled. Henry could put a mark on the wall for that one, he thought. He'd even the score one of these days.

In the meantime, he strode on toward Cherry Creek and told himself that he didn't much care what Billy Vail or the commissioner of the Mounties said about it. He was an American, by Godfrey, and he wasn't going to take orders from no redcoat! Seemed to him like they'd fought a war over that very thing, a while back . . .

Like most places in the West, you couldn't get to where Longarm was going in a straight line. He took the railroad from Denver to Cheyenne, then west to Salt Lake City, where he made connections with the Utah & Northern and headed north into Montana Territory. The railroad hadn't been completed for very long. Every station where the train stopped still had the smell of new lumber about it.

Montana was vast, open country for the most part. A few pockets of civilization in the southwest part of the territory, around the old mining camps of Bannack and Virginia City, had been settled for quite a while. Fort Benton, up on the Missouri River, had been there even longer. But it had been only a few years since George Custer and the boys of the Seventh Cavalry had met their untimely end on the hills above the Greasy Grass, better known to whites as the Little Big Horn River, and an even shorter time since Chief Joseph and the Nez Percé had surrendered to the Army, to fight no more.

The Sioux and their allies had retreated north above the Canadian border, and from what Longarm had heard, they were behaving themselves up there. Once the threat of the Indians was gone for the most part, folks had turned their eyes toward Montana Territory and had seen a land of promise. Texas cattlemen started trailing their herds north, intent on starting new ranches on the sweeping, thick-grassed plains. The Army established new forts near the border to make sure the Sioux and the other tribes didn't decide to come back across the border and raise hell again. Montana began to show signs of becoming a pretty nice place to live, and as the population grew, so did the calls for statehood. That was still a ways in the future, Longarm suspected, but it was inevitable.

The railroad came to an end at Helena, the territorial capital that had started life as the mining camp known as Last Chance Gulch. From there Longarm caught the stagecoach to Fort Shaw.

On the Sun River, west of its junction with the Missouri, Fort Shaw was considered one of the finest of the frontier forts despite its relatively isolated location. Officers with families were especially eager to be posted there, because the quarters for them bordered on luxurious compared to other forts. There were actual houses made of planks rather than the usual crude log cabins, and each house had a small yard with a fence in front of it. An officer's wife could even plant a flower bed if she wanted to. It was no wonder that Fort Shaw was sometimes called the Queen of the Montana Forts.

When you got right down to it, though, the fort existed because the frontier was still a dangerous place at times. Longarm saw plenty of rifle-toting soldiers when he stepped down from the stagecoach after it had rocked to a stop in front of regimental headquarters.

A stiff-backed lieutenant stood on the porch of the headquarters building, watching the passengers disembark from the stagecoach. Longarm's only two companions inside the coach on the journey from Helena had been a couple of drummers, one in ladies' wear and one in cooking utensils, who wanted to sell their wares to the ladies of the post. In his brown tweed suit, Longarm thought the lieutenant might take him for a drummer too, although he certainly hoped not. The Stetson and the high-topped black boots, not to mention the Colt .45 in the cross-draw rig on his left hip, ought to set him apart from those traveling salesmen.

Sure enough, the lieutenant came down the steps from the porch, approached Longarm, and extended his hand. "Marshal Long? I'm Lieutenant Phillip Stack. We got a wire telling us to expect you."

Longarm shook hands with the young officer. "Pleased to meet you, Lieutenant."

"Come inside and I'll introduce you to the post commander, Colonel Whalen."

The colonel was a short, stocky man with thinning brown hair and an aggressive brush of a mustache. He shook hands with Longarm too, and motioned the big lawman into a chair in front of his desk.

"You've come up here to look into the matter of these missing women, I understand."

"That's right." Longarm slipped a cheroot from his vest pocket. Colonel Whalen struck a wooden match and lit the cheroot with it, then used the same match to set fire to the tobacco in the bowl of his briar pipe. In a moment the air was satisfactorily blue with smoke.

Whalen sighed. "It's a terrible business. Two of the girls came from a family right here at the post, daughters of one of my officers. Carolyn and Laura McKenzie. Sisters, you know. Sixteen and eighteen."

"How'd they come to disappear?"

"They rode out into the countryside to have a picnic."

Longarm frowned. "Without an escort? I didn't reckon Montana Territory was quite *that* safe yet."

"It's not." Colonel Whalen sounded irritated. "And they had an enlisted man with them to watch out for them."

"What happened to him?" Longarm didn't recall reading anything in the reports about any men being attacked or killed in conjunction with the disappearances of the women.

"The young women decided to bathe in the river." Whalen's voice sounded stiff and uncomfortable now. "Naturally the trooper gave them some privacy. He was well within earshot, however, and heard nothing to indicate that there was any trouble. When quite some time went by, he called out to the McKenzie girls, and when they didn't answer, he investigated. They were gone, along with their clothes and their horses."

Longarm's frown deepened as he thought about what the colonel had just told him. He knew soldiers fairly well, having been one himself at one time and having worked with plenty of them since. It was a lot to ask of a fella to expect him not to sneak a peek while two nubile girls in their teens were cavorting in the altogether in a river. Maybe the trooper had seen something and was afraid to

15

say anything about it because that would mean admitting that he had spied on his female charges.

"You trust this enlisted man?"

Whalen sat up straighter in his chair. "Private Delahanty has been in the Army for over twenty years. He served with distinction during the war and has been a fine soldier in the years since then. I do trust him, Marshal."

"Well, I'll take your word for it, Colonel. No disrespect intended, but I'll want to talk with him anyway, just to hear his version of what happened."

"Of course. That's fine—"

Whalen stopped short as a commotion broke out in the adjutant's office, outside the commander's office. Longarm heard a yell. "Damn it, let go of me!"

Then there was the sound of a fist striking flesh, and a second later the door of the colonel's office was flung open as a wild-eyed man charged through it.

Chapter 3

Colonel Whalen surged to his feet. "Captain McKenzie! What's the meaning of this?"

The man stood there, knobby fists clenched at his sides, breathing heavily through gritted teeth, his rawboned face red with anger.

"I've heard that a lawman's come to look for my girls." The captain's voice held more than a touch of a Scots burr, probably made more pronounced than usual by his emotional upheaval. "Is that true, Colonel?"

Whalen ignored the question and asked one of his own. "Did you actually strike Lieutenant Stack?"

"He would'na get outta my way—"

The young lieutenant who had met Longarm at the stage appeared in the doorway between the offices, rubbing an obviously sore jaw. "Colonel, I've been attacked!"

"I can see that," Whalen said in an impatient growl. "McKenzie, explain yourself!"

The redheaded captain trembled slightly, a sign of the effort it cost him to control himself. "I heard that a federal lawman was going to conduct an investigation into my daughters' disappearance. There's a rumor going around that he just arrived on the stagecoach." McKenzie looked at Longarm. "Is this the man?"

Longarm figured the best thing to do might be to introduce himself. He said, "I'm Deputy U.S. Marshal Custis Long. And that's right, Captain, I'm here to find out what happened to your daughters, and to nearly a dozen other women in recent weeks."

McKenzie put his hands over his face, shuddered, and sank into the other straight-backed chair in front of the desk. "Thank God, thank God." The muttered words were muffled by his hands.

His anger fading, Whalen came around the desk and clasped a hand on McKenzie's shoulder. "Take it easy, Captain. We all know how upset you are."

From the doorway, the adjutant protested, "Sir, I was struck—"

"I know that, Lieutenant Stack. But I think we can make allowances under the circumstances, don't you?"

Stack looked like he would have rather demanded that McKenzie be court-martialed, but after a moment he sighed. "I suppose if you say so, sir."

"I do say so. That'll be all, Lieutenant."

So far, Longarm hadn't been particularly impressed with Whalen, but the colonel went up a notch in his estimation now. Whalen could have been a stickler for rules and regulations and thrown McKenzie into the guardhouse for walloping a fellow officer. Longarm had known plenty of by-the-book martinets who would have done just that. Instead, Whalen had taken a more reasonable course.

The colonel went back behind his desk. "It's time to pull yourself together, Captain. That's the best way you can help your daughters."

"I suppose you're right, sir." McKenzie took a deep, ragged breath and looked at Longarm. "What can I do to help, Marshal?"

Longarm's answer was blunt. "Don't lose your temper when I ask the questions I got to ask."

"All right. Go ahead."

"Is there any reason those gals of yours might've run away on their own?"

McKenzie shook his head. "No, none at all. They were happy, cheerful children."

"They liked living on an Army post?"

"Yes, of course."

"Got along all right with you and your wife?"

McKenzie's head bobbed up and down. "Yes."

"Do you have any other young'uns?"

"Another daughter and two sons. All of them younger than Carolyn and Laura."

Longarm thought for a moment about how to phrase his next question. "When gals get to be a certain age, they start to take an interest in young fellas. There's a bunch of soldiers around this fort, and a girl might think they were pretty handsome in their uniforms."

Without hesitation, McKenzie shook his head. "You have it backwards, Marshal. My daughters are quite attractive, and I won't deny that the young, unmarried officers might have cast an eye in their direction with the idea of courting them, but nothing of the sort had happened yet."

"Your oldest daughter . . ."

"Laura."

Longarm nodded. "Laura is eighteen, right?"

"Aye, that's correct."

"Out here on the frontier, lots of gals are married and have families by the time they're eighteen. It'd be sort of unusual if Laura hadn't at least thought about getting hitched before now."

McKenzie's already florid face flushed a little more. "You'd have to speak to my wife about that . . . the girls might have confided more in her than in me about such

19

matters . . . but to the best of my knowledge, Marshal, neither Laura nor Carolyn had any romantic entanglements that might have prompted them to . . . run off."

"All right. I'm obliged to you for letting me speak plain, Captain."

"I just want you to find my girls. They're all that's important."

Longarm saw the wretched pain in McKenzie's eyes as the captain stared at him. "I'll sure do my best."

That was a promise he intended to keep.

Private Finn Delahanty was a thick-necked, bald-headed Irishman who had been promoted to corporal and busted back to private dozens of times over his career. His basic competence led to the promotions, and the fights that his temper invariably caused led to the demotions. But Longarm could tell by talking to him and looking at him that Delahanty was a good, honest soldier.

"No, sir, Marshal, I didn't see a thing. Those girls were there, a-talkin' and a-laughin' so's I could hear 'em, and then after a while they wasn't no more."

"You didn't go check on them first thing when you couldn't hear them anymore?"

Delahanty shook his bullet-shaped head. "No, sir. I thought maybe they was a-layin' out on the riverbank, dryin' off after their swim. The sun was bright, and it was plenty warm enough for that." A flush spread across his bald scalp. "I didn't want to accidentally see anything I wasn't supposed to see, sir."

Longarm and the trooper stood on the porch of the sutler's store, where Longarm had found Delahanty. "You sure about that, Private?" The lawman lowered his voice to a conspiratorial tone and continued. "I hear tell those McKenzie gals are right pretty. It wouldn't have been hard for you to sneak a look, now would it?"

The muscles in Delahanty's jaws bulged as he ground

his teeth together. "Beggin' the marshal's pardon, sir, but if I wasn't under orders to cooperate, I'd be bustin' ye in the chops right about now."

"Take it easy, Delahanty." Longarm's grin took any sting out of the words. "I believe you. I just had to be sure you were telling the truth."

"Oh." Delahanty frowned. "Well, I'm still bein' offended, but in that case, I reckon it's all right."

"I suppose you took a good look around for horse tracks or anything else that might have told you somebody else was there along the river."

"Aye, first thing. I didn't find any sign except for a few hoofprints left by the girls' mounts."

"What about Indians?"

Delahanty shook his head. "There are a few tame ones around, of course, but there ain't been any hostiles in this area for months now."

Longarm frowned, tugged at his right earlobe, and then ran a thumbnail along his jawline, old habits that he displayed when he was deep in thought. Sometimes Indians only wanted you to think they were tame, but these disappearances didn't really strike him as the work of hostiles. If that had been the case, at least one of the missing women should have shown up as a scalped and mutilated corpse, although of course it was possible that all of them were still alive and being held as slaves. Indians were impatient with recalcitrant captives, however, and surely some of the missing women would have kicked up enough of a fuss so that they would be killed.

It seemed much more likely to Longarm that white men were responsible for the disappearances. Despite his questions to Captain McKenzie about whether his daughters would have run off on their own, Longarm didn't consider that a serious possibility. Twelve women and girls vanishing into thin air meant foul play.

And the foulest play he could think of was white slavery.

21

The missing women could have been kidnapped, taken somewhere else, and forced into prostitution. According to Captain McKenzie, Carolyn and Laura were both attractive. Not that such a consideration really mattered. As long as they were female, there were gents who would pay good money to bed them. Some places on the frontier, women were still so rare that they would fetch a premium price.

The idea was an ugly, dirty, low-down one, but Longarm knew there were men who would stoop that low and even lower. Unless and until he found out different, he thought that was the most likely theory.

Delahanty was worried. "You think you'll find those gals, Marshal? I hate like hell that they disappeared when I was supposed to be watchin' 'em."

"I reckon you did your best, trooper. I'll find them if anybody can."

The stage line ended at Fort Shaw, but Colonel Whalen was happy to provide Longarm with a horse and saddle. With the reports Billy Vail had given him and a map of the Montana Territory, Longarm sketched out a route that would take him from Fort Shaw to Fort Benton to Fort Assiniboine, near the Canadian border, with stops along the way at the settlements where some of the other women had disappeared. He changed into range clothes, packed his saddlebags with provisions from the sutler's store, snugged his Winchester in the saddle scabbard, and rode northeast from Fort Shaw the next morning.

Before the day was over he found himself paralleling the Missouri River. The Big Muddy didn't really deserve that name in these parts. It was fairly narrow and fast-flowing, so the water wasn't all that muddy. In earlier years there had been brisk steamboat traffic up the Missouri to Fort Benton, which was downriver from here, still a ways north and east of Longarm's location. Steamboats still plied the waters of the Missouri, and from Fort Benton

22

smaller vessels carried goods and supplies to the settlements farther upstream, like the one Longarm rode into late that afternoon.

Vengo consisted of one street that ran for several blocks from the boat landing until it petered out on the trackless plains. Not far in the distance across the river rose the foothills of a small chain of mountains known as the Highwood Range.

The settlement boasted of two stores, three saloons, a wagon yard and blacksmith shop, and a church that doubled as a school for several months out of the year, whenever the ranchers in the area could be bothered to send their kids into town for a rudimentary education. Mostly the ranchers and the cowboys who worked for them counted on Vengo more for supplies and whiskey.

The schoolteacher was the reason Longarm was here, though. Her name was Abbie Channing, and she was one of the women who had turned up missing.

Vengo was supposed to have a marshal, but Longarm didn't hunt up the local lawman. The time had come for him to start being more discreet in his investigation. He headed for one of the saloons instead, a rambling log structure with a sign over its entrance that read ALAMO SALOON. Down in Abilene, Kansas, there had been a famous Alamo Saloon, called that to attract the business of the thousands of Texans who had driven herds of longhorns to the railhead. No doubt a similar theory was at work here in Vengo. Many of the cattlemen and the punchers who worked for them had come to Montana Territory from Texas. The owner of this Alamo Saloon probably wanted to lure them by reminding them of their home.

Since it was summer, the door of the saloon was open. Longarm stepped into the shadowy interior and let his eyes rove around the room. A card game was in progress at one of the roughly made tables, and three men stood at the bar that had been constructed by laying thick, heavy planks

23

across three whiskey barrels spaced about six feet apart. The bartender had a bushy beard and sported a dirty gray apron over greasy buckskins. A battered silk top hat with an eagle feather stuck in the band perched on his tangled thatch of gray hair. He motioned Longarm over to the bar.

"What's your poison, stranger? We got the finest hooch in Montana, guaranteed no black powder nor rattlesnake venom in our whiskey."

"Well, if it's that good, old son, I'll just have to try it." Longarm dropped a coin on the bar.

The bartender waved a hand over the coin but left it lying there. "First one's on the house. Once you taste it, though, you'll be buyin' another."

"Sounds fair to me."

The man in the top hat poured amber liquid from a bottle into a fairly clean glass and slid it across to Longarm. With one quick motion, Longarm tossed back the drink and waited for fire to explode in his belly.

The whiskey went down surprisingly smoothly, and although it was potent, the kick wasn't as raw as some. The bartender had made good on his boast. Longarm nodded for a refill.

One of the other drinkers walked over to him, spurs jingling. He wore a black vest and black leather cuffs over a faded blue shirt, and his round-crowned, round-brimmed black hat was pushed far back on his head. He regarded Longarm with interest.

"Lookin' for a ridin' job, friend?"

Longarm inclined his head. "I might be."

"Name's Lehane. I'm foreman for Randolph Hale, up from the Nueces country in Texas. Got the RH spread up here now. It ain't really the right time of year to be hirin' grub-line riders, but if you want, you can ride on out to the ranch and tell the boss I said for you to talk to him about a job."

Longarm nodded. "I'm obliged, hombre. I might just do that."

Lehane jerked his head at the other two men, who were obviously RH punchers as well. The three of them left the Alamo Saloon.

The bartender in the silk top hat watched them go. "You caught Buck Lehane on a good day, mister. A lot of the time he's spoilin' for a fight."

"Oh? Why's that?"

"His sweetheart up and left him. Gal who taught school here in the winter. Buck figured they was gonna get hitched, but instead she run off."

"Do tell? What was her name?"

If the bartender thought that was an odd question for a stranger in town to be asking, he gave no sign of it. "Miss Channing. Abbie Channing."

Longarm knew the name, of course. It was on one of those reports he had squirreled away in his saddlebags.

Chapter 4

"Anybody know what happened to her?" Longarm tried to make the question sound just idly curious.

The bartender shook his head. "Nope. One mornin', she just didn't show up for her job clerkin' at Dugan's store. That's what she did while she wasn't teachin' school. Folks went to the cabin where she lived on the edge of town, and everything looked like it ought to. All her belongin's were there. But Miss Channing wasn't."

"That's mighty strange." Longarm frowned as he sipped from the second drink the bartender had poured for him.

The man shrugged. "I reckon. Seems like if she'd planned to leave Vengo, she would've packed up her stuff and took it with her. Ain't sure how she would've left anyway. There's no stagecoach or train. She come to town in a buggy, but it and her horse are still down at the livery stable. The old fella who runs the place ain't quite sure what to do with them."

"Well, that's mighty odd, but it ain't none o' my business." Longarm frowned as if a thought had just occurred to him. "Say, you don't think that Lehane fella could've done something to her, do you? Maybe they got in some sort of fight, and he lost his temper. . . ."

The bartender was already shaking his head. "You don't know Buck Lehane. He worshipped the ground that gal walked on, and he didn't have any trouble with his temper before she disappeared. That's what's changed him. He'd have sooner cut off his own arm with a rusty pocketknife than harmed Miss Channing."

"I reckon I can see why he's so upset then."

"You gonna ride out to the RH and ask for a job?"

"Maybe. It's late, though. I suppose I'll wait until tomorrow. Any place in town I can get a room for the night?"

The bartender jerked a thumb over his shoulder. "There's a couple of rooms in the back o' this place that I rent out to pilgrims. Ain't fancy, but the bunks beat sleepin' on the ground."

"I'll take one." Longarm got a calculating look on his face. "A gent wouldn't be able to get a mite of feminine companionship in this settlement, would he?"

With a mournful look on his face, the bartender shook his head. "Sorry, mister. You won't find a whore closer'n Fort Benton."

"Well, I guess I'll have to wait." Longarm shrugged. "I'll live."

The bartender showed him to the room, which was small, cramped, and none too clean. The straw mattress on the bunk didn't have any bedbugs, though, so Longarm spent a fairly comfortable night there, and was back on the trail early the next morning after sharing breakfast with the Alamo's proprietor.

He didn't head for the RH ranch, however, but followed the Missouri River instead. By nightfall he reached Fort Benton.

As the oldest military installation in the territory, Fort Benton consisted not only of the Army post but also a good-sized civilian settlement that had grown up around it. Four women had vanished from Fort Benton. One was a soldier's wife; the other three had no connection with the

Army as far as Longarm knew. He had practically memorized the reports by now, knew all the names and backgrounds of the missing women. When he entered the town and drew even with a large, barnlike building, he reined his horse toward the open doors. A sign over those doors read DOWLING FREIGHT.

Longarm swung down from the saddle. Holding the horse's reins, he called into the cavernous building, "Anybody home?"

A moment later, a surly reply came back. "Hold your damn horses."

Longarm glanced at his mount and thought that was exactly what he was doing, but he kept that comment to himself. A man walked out of the shadows, his gait a little unsteady, and stopped to regard Longarm with an unfriendly glare.

"What is it you want, mister?"

"You the owner of this freight line?"

"That's right. Name's Ben Dowling. What do you want?" the man asked again.

Ben Dowling was none too friendly, and none too sober, either, thought Longarm. His nose was red and bulbous over a thick sandy mustache. He sniffed and swayed a little as he glowered at Longarm.

"Thought you might be hiring drivers."

Dowling sniffed again. "You look more like a cowboy than a teamster."

"I can handle a team, don't you worry about that, Mr. Dowling."

The freight line owner waved a hand. "Well, I don't need any drivers. Get the hell outta here."

Longarm frowned and said, "No call to be unfriendly about it, just because you ain't hiring right now."

"I'll be unfriendly if I want to." Dowling stepped forward, his big hands clenching into fists at his side. "Now go on and don't bother me again, you no-good saddle tramp."

Longarm wasn't going to push the matter. He hadn't come here to fight. But before he could back off and leave the freight barn, a man walking along the street nearby spoke up, saying, "Take it easy, Ben. I don't think this fella is looking for trouble."

"Then he better move along."

Longarm spoke to the other man, who wore a dusty gray suit and had a badge pinned to his vest. "That's just what I was about to do, Marshal."

The local lawman nodded. "Much obliged, mister. I'll walk with you, if that's all right."

"Sure."

Still leading his horse, Longarm started along the street. A glance over his shoulder showed him Ben Dowling turning and making his unsteady way back into the barn.

"That hombre's sure got a burr up his backside," Longarm said. The comment was uttered in a low voice, intended only for the ears of the marshal.

"It's a sad case." The marshal shook his head. "Ben's wife disappeared a few weeks ago. He hasn't been the same since."

"Disappeared? How do you mean?"

"Just up and vanished. He walked home from his business one day and Julie wasn't there. Nobody had any clue what had happened to her."

Longarm grunted. "Now that's mighty strange."

The marshal was in late middle age, with gray hair and a lined, weathered face. He looked every one of his years. The trouble in Fort Benton was obviously weighing on him.

"It's even worse than that," he said. "Julie Dowling isn't the only woman who's gone missing hereabouts. Four ladies have vanished in the past couple of months."

"It don't sound like it's very safe around here. Maybe I'd better move on, instead of looking for a job."

The marshal looked over at Longarm as they walked

along. The afternoon light had started to fade. Soon it would be dusk.

"Just what *is* your business in Fort Benton, Mister . . . ?"

"Parker. And I'm just drifting, looking for work when the mood strikes me. Nothing that's going to last too long, though."

"Fiddle-footed, eh? I've seen a lot just like you, Parker." The marshal didn't sound so friendly now. "Maybe you're right. Maybe you ought to move on."

"Come morning, I probably will." Longarm turned to look back at the freight barn. "How do you know that fella didn't do something to his wife? He seems like he's got a mighty short fuse."

"No chance of that. Julie Dowling is young and pretty. She's Ben's second wife. He wouldn't have hurt a hair on her head."

"Young, pretty wife married to an older gent . . . sometimes that's a cause for trouble right there."

The marshal looked and sounded disgusted as he said, "Don't you go spreading rumors like that while you're here. I'll throw you in the hoosegow if you do."

"On what charge?"

"Annoying the hell out of somebody you hadn't ought to."

Longarm couldn't help but chuckle. "Don't worry, Marshal. I was just woolgathering. Whatever happened to Mrs. Dowling, it's none of my business and I intend to keep it that way."

"See that you do."

The marshal went on his way, and Longarm stopped at a saloon. The local lawman probably would have been a lot friendlier if Longarm had shown him the leather folder that contained his badge and bona fides, but it didn't really matter. Longarm had found out what he wanted to know about Julie Dowling's disappearance. Her husband could be pretty well ruled out as a suspect. That left Longarm back where he had started, with the theory that the missing women were being abducted and sold as prostitutes.

He spent the evening drifting from saloon to saloon, doing a little talking and a lot of listening. As always, saloons were good places to pick up information, and Fort Benton was buzzing with talk about the missing women. All the ladies at the post were staying very close to home these days, as were the women who lived in the civilian settlement. The fear was pervasive among them that one of them might be the next to vanish.

The gossip followed the same pattern that Longarm had heard so far in this case: Vera Malone, wife of Army Lieutenant Douglas Malone, had disappeared while she was out riding alone. She had been the first woman to vanish around here, so no one had been taking any special precautions at that time. The twenty-year-old daughter of the local preacher had been the next to drop out of sight; at that age she was considered something of an old maid, but she was attractive enough, from what Longarm heard. Next to go had been Julie Dowling, and finally sixteen-year-old Emily Sue Preston, whose mother was a seamstress and evidently something of a harridan.

Longarm was just curious enough about the Preston girl and her circumstances so that he sought out her mother the next morning, riding up to a small house on the edge of the settlement and dismounting with a small package in his hand.

A woman with tightly braided salt-and-pepper hair and a severe expression answered Longarm's knock on the door. "Yes? What can I do for you?"

"Folks tell me you're a seamstress, ma'am?"

"That's right."

Longarm held out the package in his hand. "I got a shirt here with a big rip in it that needs mending." That was the truth. He had put the rip in his spare shirt that very morning, before leaving the hotel where he had spent the night.

Mrs. Agatha Preston glared at him. "I make dresses, young man. I don't mend cowboys' shirts. You'll have to either do it yourself or find some painted jezebel to take care of it for you."

"But sewing is sewing, ain't it? And I never was much of a hand at delicate work like that."

Now that was a blatant falsehood—as a veteran frontiersman Longarm was the master of many skills, and he could handle a needle and thread just fine—but Mrs. Preston didn't have to know that. He thought she was starting to waver, so he continued his assault.

"Besides, I never did like to associate with women of the sort you mentioned, ma'am. I'm just naturally more comfortable around decent, God-fearing women like yourself."

She frowned at him. "Who told you about me, sir?"

"Why, I believe it was the marshal . . . or maybe the local pastor, I sort of disremember."

"Reverend Williams *has* been known to say that I'm one of the leading lights of his flock." She hesitated only a moment longer before stepping back. "Come in, sir. I'll mend your shirt."

"Thank you kindly, ma'am." Longarm gave her the wrapped-up shirt and stepped into a fussily neat parlor.

"Sit down. I'll be right back."

Longarm took off his Stetson and lowered himself carefully onto a spindly chair. He was a big man, and he didn't want to break it. Mrs. Preston returned a moment later with a sewing bag and took a seat across from Longarm.

"You didn't tell me your name, sir."

"It's Parker, ma'am. Custis Parker."

"I'm pleased to meet you." She studied the rip in the shirt and then took out a needle and some thread. With an ease born of long practice, she slipped the thread through the eye of the needle. "It's always good to make the acquaintance of a decent gentleman. Most of the men around here are nothing but crude, godless louts."

"Well, I suppose they're just not strong enough to resist all the temptation that's placed in their path, ma'am."

She snorted. "Nonsense! A good man is always able to resist temptation. That's what makes him a good man. I've seen plenty of the other kind, though, starting with my husband."

"I was under the impression from what I heard that you were a widow, ma'am."

"Might as well be."

Longarm wasn't sure what she meant by that, but he wanted to bring the conversation around to a more pertinent subject.

"I'm really sorry to hear about your loss, too. Must be mighty hard."

Mrs. Preston had started mending the rip in the shirt. Her fingers faltered a little, though, as Longarm spoke. She glanced up at him.

"You've heard the gossip, I suppose. About Emily Sue, I mean."

"I, uh, heard that something had happened to her . . ."

"She was taken from me."

"By the Lord, you mean?"

"By someone. Certainly not the Lord. Probably by one of those awful cowboys who came around here trying to court her."

"Popular with the boys, was she?"

Mrs. Preston looked up sharply at him. "What do you mean by that?"

Longarm held up his hands, palms out. "No offense meant, ma'am, none at all. I just thought . . . Well, I heard that your Emily Sue was a mighty pretty girl—"

"She's a good girl, that's what she is. I saw to that. I never allowed a single evil thought into that girl's head. Why, anytime I even suspected that she as much as smiled at a boy, I took a strap to her and locked her in her room. She's pure, unsullied, and I intend to see that she stays that way! I mean, I intended . . . I only wanted . . . but she's not here anymore, and I . . . I can't . . ."

She dropped the shirt and the needle and thread into her lap, and her hands came up to cover her face as sobs began to shake her angular body. Longarm felt lower than a snake's belly for steering the conversation to this point. But he had wanted to find out just what sort of life Emily Sue Preston led here in Fort Benton, and now he had a pretty good idea. Of all the disappearances he had investigated so far, he thought this one was the most likely to be a case where the girl had simply run away.

But it was equally possible that whoever had abducted the other women had grabbed Emily Sue as well. Until Longarm knew differently, he had to consider her disappearance to be part of the same case as the others.

"Ma'am, I sure didn't mean to upset you. You don't have to finish mending that shirt—"

Mrs. Preston sniffled. "Nonsense. I always finish the jobs I start." She picked up the shirt and got back to work on it. "A workman is worthy of his hire, it says in the Good Book, and so is a woman."

"Yes, ma'am. And I know what you mean about finishing what you start."

That was exactly what Longman intended to do. He would stay on the trail until he had found those missing women . . . or at least until he'd found out what had happened to them, and had brought justice to the sorry bastards who were responsible for it.

Chapter 5

From Fort Benton, Longarm moved on to a settlement called Elktooth, where he got his first real break in the case. Helen Baxter, the twenty-four-year-old sister of the local storekeeper, was the woman who had disappeared from Elktooth. Grant Baxter was still broken up about it, and he was more than willing to talk when Longarm stopped in at the store to pick up a few supplies.

"I didn't like the way they were looking at her," the balding Baxter said as he got a box of .44 cartridges down from a shelf and put it on the counter in front of Longarm. "There were two of them, rough-looking gents. One wore a buffalo coat, and the other one, the little one, had a derby hat. I noticed the fella in the coat first. It gets cool at night up here, even in the summer, but it isn't really the time of year for somebody to be sporting a coat like that."

"They came into the store the same day your sis disappeared?" Longarm asked. He didn't have to be subtle here; Baxter was eager to talk.

The storekeeper nodded. "That's right. It was about an hour before dark. I remember it well. They said they were on their way to Fort Assiniboine, that they worked for the

Army as teamsters. I didn't really believe them, though. I thought even then that they were up to no good."

"What happened then?"

"Well, like I said, they . . . they *looked* at Helen. Now, I suppose my sister is no raving beauty, but she's a handsome woman, handsome enough so that she's been walking out in the evening with both Noah Fordwick at the livery stable and Doc Brant from the barbershop. I suspect she would have married one of them before too much longer, if she'd ever made up her mind. Now, though . . ." Baxter shook his head and his voice caught a little as he went on. "Now I don't know what's become of her."

"I'm mighty sorry," Longarm said, and meant it. "But back to these fellas who came in that day . . ."

"Oh, yeah, them. They looked at Helen and talked to her a little, but that was nothing unusual, as I was saying. Then they got in their wagon and drove off, and I didn't really think about them again until later, after Helen vanished on her way home."

Baxter continued the story, telling Longarm that it was his habit to keep the store open for an hour or so after dark each day in case there were any late customers. Helen usually left around sundown, though, and walked the two blocks to the house she shared with her brother, where she would prepare supper so that it would be ready when he got home after closing the store.

But on the night in question, Baxter had gone home to a dark, empty house. Helen had never reached it after leaving the store.

"Right away, I thought of those two," Baxter said. "I thought they must have slipped back and waited for her, then grabbed her and carried her off to do . . . to do God knows what to her." He shuddered.

Longarm reached across the counter and clasped his arm. "Take it easy, old son. Maybe it ain't as bad as you think."

"Then what other explanation could there be? You tell me that, sir."

Longarm had no answer for the distraught man. But he had a lead at last, maybe.

"You didn't hear those two hombres call each other by name while they were in your store, did you?"

Baxter shook his head. "Not that I recall."

"Did you tell the law about them?"

"A deputy sheriff came by a week or so later," Baxter said with a sigh. "I told him about my suspicions and he promised he would look into it, but I doubt if he ever did. There's not much law up here yet, mister, and what there is of it is stretched mighty thin. I hope it'll be different one of these days when Montana becomes a state."

"More than likely," Longarm said. "What did they look like, besides the buffalo coat and the derby hat, I mean?"

Baxter frowned as he looked across the counter. "You're asking so many questions it almost sounds to me like *you're* a lawman."

Longarm shook his head. "Not hardly. It's just that I'm riding on up toward Fort Assiniboine myself, and I thought I'd keep my eyes open for those two varmints. If I see 'em, maybe I can get the Army to arrest them and find out where your sister is."

Hope sprang to life in Baxter's eyes. He said, "The one in the buffalo coat was big, every bit as tall as you and a good bit wider. He wore a black hat with a big brim and had sandy-colored hair and a beard. The one with the derby was only about half the size of his partner and had a face like a fox. Wore a little goatee, too. He did most of the talking. I don't think the big one was too bright."

"Sounds like I ought to know them if I see them, all right."

"Yeah, you'll recognize them. I don't think there are too many gents around who look like that."

Baxter might have been surprised about that—the descrip-

39

tions didn't really sound all that distinctive to Longarm—but they were good enough so that he was confident he would know the men if he ran across them.

"You say they had a wagon?"

"Yeah, sort of like a mud wagon, only with closed sides. Like a medicine show wagon, come to think of it."

"Did you see any writing on it?"

Baxter shook his head. "If there was, I didn't notice it. But I don't really think anything was written on it."

"All right," Longarm said. "I'll sure keep my eyes open."

"Anything you can do to help find Helen, I'll really appreciate it, mister." Baxter gave a mournful sigh. "I sure would like to have her back. We been on our own since we were youngsters, back in Illinois. Our folks died, so we always had to look out for each other."

"You must not have been too happy then about the idea of your sister maybe getting hitched to one of her beaus."

"No, you've got that wrong," Baxter said without hesitation. "I just wanted Helen to be happy, that's all. If she'd have gotten married and raised a passel of kids, it would have been just fine with me." He sighed again. "Not much chance of that happening now, though."

"You never know about things like that, old son," Longarm told him. "Best to eat the apple one bite at a time and not get ahead of yourself."

"Problem is," Baxter said, "ever since poor Helen disappeared, that apple has gone downright sour."

Longarm wished he had the time to double back to the places he'd already been and find out if those two gents and their wagon had been seen in the vicinity of the other disappearances. He knew, though, that with every day that went by, the situation in which those missing women found themselves might be getting more desperate.

Even though he had no proof, the instincts he had developed over the years as a lawman told him that the two men Baxter had mentioned were responsible for those girls and women vanishing. They might have been traveling around Montana Territory for weeks, looking for women attractive enough to fetch a good price when they were sold into prostitution. They probably kept their captives in that closed-up wagon. More than likely the women had been tied up, gagged, maybe even drugged to keep them docile.

But what was the kidnappers' destination? Where were they headed with their prisoners? As he rode north toward Fort Assinniboine, Longarm thought back over everything he had gleaned from the reports, including the dates that the women had gone missing. It was obvious the kidnappers were working their way north.

Canada?

Billy Vail had said that this job might take Longarm across the border. Vail had been a star-packer for a lot more years than Longarm, and he had the same sort of instincts. Vail had picked up on the Canadian possibility just by reading through the reports. Longarm was convinced that the hunch he shared with the chief marshal was correct.

He made one more stop before he reached Fort Assiniboine, at a trading post called Eli's Crossing. A seventeen-year-old girl had disappeared from the trading post while the immigrant family she belonged to had been stopped there overnight. The rest of the family had pushed on to Oregon after several days of searching for the missing girl had failed to turn up any signs of her. It must have been hard for her parents and brothers and sisters to leave her there like that, Longarm thought, but they hadn't had much choice in the matter.

The trading post was run by a man named Eli Miller. Stocky and sandy-haired, he had a trace of a British accent. Longarm wasn't surprised when Miller mentioned that he had come down to Montana Territory from Canada.

"I'm thinkin' I might go back, though," Miller said as he

and Longarm sat on stools by a cracker barrel and sipped from cups of coffee. "The Mounted Police have the Indians under control, and once the railroad comes through, the western provinces will explode with growth. A man could make a pretty penny by bein' in the right place at the right time."

"That's the Canadian Pacific you're talking about?"

"Of course. It'll stretch all the way to the coast, unless I miss my guess."

Longarm nodded slowly and thought Miller was right. There had been talk for years of building a transcontinental railroad across Canada, like the Union Pacific and the Central Pacific that had linked up the east and west coasts of the United States. Now construction had begun, and the steel rails were advancing steadily across the plains toward the Rockies.

One thing was certain about a railroad: It took a lot of men to build one. And wherever there were a lot of men, there would be a heavy demand for women. Longarm sipped his coffee and thought about that. If somebody had a dozen young, attractive women working for him as whores, he could make a fortune just by following the railhead. Women would be few and far between on the Canadian frontier; pretty ones would be even rarer.

"When that poor immigrant gal disappeared, do you remember if there was another wagon around the same day?" he asked Miller.

The trading post owner scratched his head in thought. "Well, maybe. Now that you mention it, I think there was. A couple of gents in a wagon stopped by late that afternoon, I think. They moved on, though, and I never saw them again."

"Big fella in a buffalo coat, and a little fella in a derby hat?"

Miller's eyes widened. "Say, that's right! Are they friends of yours?"

"Not hardly," Longarm said with a shake of his head. "They left while the girl and her family were still here?"

"That's right."

And then they circled back around, snuck up to the trading post after dark, and grabbed the girl, thought Longarm. Just like with Helen Baxter. They were stealthy bastards, able to slip in and out of a place without being noticed. They had to be ruthless too, because the only way they could handle their captives without the women raising a ruckus would be to knock them out right away.

Longarm was sure looking forward to catching up to them. It was going to be very satisfying to see that those two sons of bitches got what was coming to them.

"Say, you think those men might've had something to do with the girl who disappeared?" Miller asked suddenly.

"Could be. Was anybody else around that day?"

Miller shook his head. "Not so's I remember. I just never thought about them before now, because I thought they were long gone. They could have lurked around just out of sight of the place, though, until after dark."

"Yeah, that was my thought too."

"You said you're ridin' on up to the fort?"

"That's right."

"Maybe you ought to tell all this to the commanding officer up there. Might be there's something he can do about it."

"You could be right," Longarm said.

Miller frowned. "The authorities ought to know about this. Maybe that girl could still be found."

Longarm nodded. The authorities—in the person of him—already knew what was going on. And he was going to find that immigrant girl and all the other missing women. He felt that in his bones.

A day later he rode into Fort Assiniboine. The Canadian border was just a day's ride to the north. The fort, which had been constructed only recently, was the largest military installation west of the Mississippi River. All the buildings were made of bricks, and it was truly an impressive sight. There were a few Indian tipis nearby and a handful of civilian buildings, but that was the extent of the adjacent settlement. This was the last place where any women had been reported missing. Longarm recalled the details from the reports. Martha Davidge, who worked for the Army as a seamstress, mending uniforms, was one of the women who had gone missing from here. The other was Clarissa Ralston, a missionary lady who had come to Montana Territory to spread the Word of God among the Indians.

Longarm dismounted and tied his horse in front of the civilian trading post about a hundred yards from the fort. He was debating whether or not to reveal his true identity to the commanding officer as he stepped up onto the porch.

Then the door burst open in front of him and somebody came flying out to crash into him, and Longarm didn't have time to ponder anything because he was busy falling backward into the mud.

Chapter 6

The landing knocked the breath out of him, and the weight of the man who had run into him and was lying on top of him kept Longarm from getting any air. With a grunt of effort, he shoved the man to the side and rolled out from under him.

The man wound up facedown in the mud, and he didn't seem to be making any effort to lift his head from the stuff. Fearing that the man would choke to death, Longarm reached over, grabbed the back of his filthy sheepskin jacket, and pulled him up. The man's face came free from the muck with a sucking sound. His features were thickly coated with mud.

Muttering curses, Longarm pushed himself to his feet and hauled the man upright with him. There was a watering trough close by. Longarm shoved the man over to it, holding him up along the way because the man's legs constantly threatened to fold up and go out from under him. When they reached the trough, Longarm let the man fall to his knees. Then Longarm dunked his head into the water.

The man came up sputtering and blowing and cursing, but at least his mouth and nose were clear enough now so that he could get some air through them. He leaned his hands on the edge of the trough and dragged deep, ragged breaths into his body.

Longarm had caught his own breath by now. He looked down at the mud on his clothes and grimaced. The laughter that sounded from the porch of the trading post didn't improve his mood any.

He looked up and saw several soldiers standing there. They were burly, rough-featured men with sergeant's stripes on their sleeves. One of them was laughing so hard that he had to wipe tears from his eyes before he was able to say to Longarm, "Sorry about the collision, mister. When we tossed that rummy out the door, we didn't know he was going to run into anybody."

Longarm jerked his head toward the man, who was still leaning over the water trough, coughing and gasping. "He could have choked to death on that mud, you know."

"Naw, we would've pulled him out before he strangled," one of the other noncoms said.

"Come on inside," the third sergeant said. "We'll buy you a drink to make up for gettin' your clothes dirty."

Longarm thought it over, but only for a moment. Sergeants, like bartenders, were usually fine sources of information. He said, "All right, but wait a minute first."

He walked over to the water trough and bent slightly to put a hand on the shoulder of the man who knelt there. "Are you gonna be all right, old son?"

The man wiped more mud away from his face with a trembling hand and then lifted his head to look up at Longarm, who was a little surprised to see that the man wasn't as old as Longarm had assumed he was. The scruffy beard and the mud smeared all over his face made him look older than he really was. In a voice thickened and roughened by raw whiskey, he said, "Y-yeah, I'm f-fine. Thanks for your help, mister."

"*De nada*. I'm not gonna stand by and watch anybody

46

choke to death on mud, not even somebody who just knocked me down."

"Wasn't my idea," the man muttered.

Longarm glanced at the three sergeants. "Yeah, I know," he said quietly. He squeezed the man's shoulder and left him kneeling there.

"We got a good laundry here," one of the noncoms said as they ushered Longarm into the trading post. "You can get those duds of yours washed up right fine."

"I'm obliged," Longarm said with a nod. Half of the sprawling trading post served as a saloon. He went to the bar with the sergeants and let them buy him a beer. The bartender filled mugs for the three soldiers as well.

As they drank, Longarm asked, "How come you tossed that fella out of here?"

"Aw, we just got tired of watching him stumble around. He ain't been sober since he rode in a week ago."

"Who is he?"

"Damned if we know. Just some drifter."

Longarm nodded. The Army was sometimes a brutal organization that attracted some brutal men. These three hadn't had any real reason for attacking the drunk other than sheer meanness. Still, even though he didn't like them, Longarm wasn't going to pass up the opportunity to maybe learn a few things from them.

"I'm surprised some psalm-singer didn't get hold of him first and try to reform him," he commented.

"Naw, the chaplain just tries to save us sinners in uniform, and there ain't no regular civilian preacher up here yet."

"No missionaries trying to see to it that Mister Lo winds up in the Kingdom of Heaven instead of the Happy Hunting Ground?"

One of the sergeants nudged the noncom beside him. "Say, there was that Ralston gal, wasn't there? How come she didn't start in on the rummy?"

47

"Because she was gone before he showed up," the second sergeant said.

"Oh. Yeah, I guess that's right. It's been almost two weeks that she's been gone, hasn't it?"

"Where'd she go?" Longarm asked innocently.

The third sergeant poked a finger against Longarm's chest. "Now that there is a good question, my friend. Nobody knows."

Longarm didn't care for being poked like that, but he didn't show his irritation. Instead, he frowned and said, "What in blazes do you mean by that?"

"Miss Ralston—the missionary lady we're talkin' about—up and disappeared one evening when she was walking back to the fort from the redskin village."

"What happened? Did the Indians get her?"

All three of the noncoms shook their heads. "Those are blanket Indians," one of them said. "They're a lot more interested in gettin' their monthly beef allotment than they are in liftin' the hair of some psalm-singin' missionary gal."

"Even when that hair is bright red like Miss Ralston's," added one of the others.

"Yeah, she'd have been mighty pretty if she'd ever taken down that long hair."

"And taken off that black dress that looked like she was goin' to a funeral. I swear, she had some mighty fine tits under there."

Longarm steered the conversation away from the physical assets of Miss Clarissa Ralston by saying, "You're telling me this gal just vanished into thin air?"

"That's exactly what we're tellin' you, friend. There were troopers on sentry duty, and they never saw or heard a thing. It's almost like she just walked out onto the prairie for some reason and never came back."

Longarm drank some more of his beer. He suspected that was pretty close to what had happened. The two men

48

he was looking for had either sneaked up close to the fort and grabbed Clarissa Ralston with the same sort of stealth and guile they had demonstrated in other places, or else they had somehow lured her farther away from the post and then kidnapped her. Either way, Longarm was confident that she had wound up in the back of that closed-up wagon with the other missing women.

He said, "A couple of friends of mine were talking about heading up this way. Maybe you fellas have seen them. One of them is a big hombre, about as tall as me, who wears a buffalo coat. The other one's more of a short-growed sort and favors a derby hat. Chances are they'd be driving a wagon."

The three noncoms frowned in thought. After a moment one of them said, "Maybe. I ain't sure, but that sounds like a couple of gents who passed through a while back."

"Yeah," confirmed another of the sergeants. "They said they were scoutin' out the lay of the land for some ranchin' syndicate. Seemed to me more likely they were smugglin' whiskey or guns in that wagon of theirs, but they didn't cause any ruckus while they were here. We didn't have any cause to search them or their wagon."

"There's talk that we're goin' to start patrollin' for smugglers and searchin' every civilian we come across, but the orders ain't come down yet."

And because of that, thought Longarm, the men had gotten away with their scheme. They were lucky as well as evil.

He reminded himself that he still had no proof the two men were behind the disappearances of the women. But he hadn't come up with any other reasonable possibilities, so for the time being he had to proceed as if that theory were correct, even though he could keep an open mind and an open pair of eyes in case anything else cropped up.

He saw that the drunk the sergeants had tossed out earlier had slunk back into the trading post and was now slumped at a table in the corner, his head down and resting on his crossed arms. As Longarm looked at him, a soft snore came from the man. Longarm hoped everyone would just let the poor bastard sleep it off.

He and the sergeants had finished their beers. One of the men said, "Come on with us, mister, and we'll take you over to the laundry. You got an extra pair of duds you can change into while those are bein' cleaned?"

"Yeah, I reckon." Longarm's brown tweed suit was folded up in his saddlebags. He could wear it.

The drunk continued snoring in the corner as Longarm and the three sergeants left the trading post.

None of them saw him lift his head from his apparent sleep and peer after them, his attention focused on the back of the tall lawman.

"Now, don't you look like a dude?" one of Longarm's new-found noncommissioned acquaintances said as Longarm walked out of the post laundry wearing his brown tweed suit and dark brown vest over a white shirt. A watch chain crossed from one vest pocket to the other, and he had even tied a string tie around his neck.

What the soldiers didn't know was that at one end of that watch chain, acting as a fob, was a deadly .41-caliber two-shot derringer. That wicked little hideout gun had saved Longarm's bacon more than once during his long and eventful career.

"You fellas just don't recognize distinguished when you see it," Longarm said.

"Distinguished," repeated one of the sergeants. "Don't that mean full of hot air and horseshit?"

Longarm grinned. "Only when it applies to politicians and generals."

The three men laughed. They had formed a bond of sorts with Longarm. That didn't stop them from being curious. One of the men said, "You know, you never told us your name, or what you're doin' here at Fort Assiniboine."

"Name's Parker," said Longarm, sticking with his usual answer when he was working undercover. "I'm part of that ranching syndicate deal my partners told you about." Since the men he was after had used that story, he thought he might as well take advantage of it.

"You mean that was the truth? They weren't really smugglers?"

"Not unless I am too," Longarm said as he took out a cheroot.

That made them frown suspiciously at him for a moment, but then one of the men shook his head and said, "The hell with that. A smuggler wouldn't come ridin' into the fort bold as brass like Parker here and his friends did. They must be tellin' the truth."

Longarm snapped a lucifer to life on an iron-hard thumbnail and held the flame to the tip of the cheroot. When he had the smoke going, he tossed the sulfur match into the mud. With a grin, he said around the cheroot, "You gents wouldn't know where a fella could find himself a little female companionship, would you?"

Surprisingly, glum expressions appeared on the faces of the three noncoms. "Not around here," one of them answered. "I hear tell there are a few whores down at Fort Benton."

That was true. Longarm hadn't patronized any of them, but he had asked enough questions to know that several ladies of the evening plied their trade in the saloons at Fort Benton. All of them had been at it for a while, though; there were no newcomers in the game, and that was all Longarm had been interested in. It told him that the women he was looking for wouldn't be found there.

One of the sergeants pointed across the plains toward the Indian village. "Some of those squaws would be willin' to bed you, Parker, if you ain't too particular about such things. They're sort of ugly and they smell of bear grease, but they're the only relief we got around here."

"I reckon I'll pass," Longarm said. He wasn't interested in Indian prostitutes either, only in fresh, young white ones.

Everything he had found out still pointed toward Canada as the destination for the kidnappers and their captives. The vast provinces of Alberta and Saskatchewan were north of the Montana border. Settlements were few and far between up there too . . . which left the railroad as the most likely place the women and girls would be put to work.

He was musing on that when one of the sergeants nudged him in the ribs with an elbow and said, "Uh-oh. Here comes trouble."

Longarm looked where the man's chin-jerk indicated and saw a lieutenant striding toward them through the dusk. The sergeants came to attention and saluted. The lieutenant, who had a narrow mustache and a prissy look about him, returned the salute and said, "At ease, men." He looked at Longarm and went on. "Welcome to Fort Assiniboine, sir. Could I trouble you to tell me who you are and what your business is here?"

There was nothing unusual about an officer keeping up with civilian visitors to the fort. This lieutenant was probably the commanding officer's adjutant. He reminded Longarm of Lieutenant Stack down at Fort Shaw. Stiff-necked, by-the-book sorts like that tended to gravitate toward such jobs.

"My name is Custis Parker, Lieutenant. I've been sent up here to Montana Territory by the ranching syndicate I work for. They're in the market for land, and it's my job to see that they make the right moves."

"I see," the lieutenant said. "I assume you have documentation of this position?"

"Not on me. It's in my saddlebags." Longarm silently muttered a curse. The sergeant had been right: This officious prig of a junior officer was trouble, no doubt about it.

Luckily, Longarm had an ace to play.

"If you'll get your paperwork and come with me, sir, we'll see the commanding officer. I'm sure you understand. There's a burgeoning traffic in guns and liquor across the border, and we have to be sure that visitors to the area are really who they say they are."

"Sure. I'll be right with you, old son."

The lieutenant sniffed, not caring for being addressed that way. Longarm didn't care. He walked across to the hitch rail where he had left his horse, took the sheaf of reports from his saddlebags, and followed the lieutenant to the headquarters building. He waved farewell to the sergeants along the way.

The lieutenant led him inside the building to an inner office. The commanding officer was working late this evening, thought Longarm. It was just about suppertime, but the hombre was still at his desk. He was a colonel with a brush of iron-gray hair and a florid face. He looked up and asked, "Who is this, Lieutenant Harper?"

"He says his name is Custis Parker, and that he works for a ranching syndicate." The lieutenant's tone indicated that he was skeptical about Longarm's claims.

And with good reason, the big lawman thought wryly, since they were both lies. The time had come, though, to lay down his cards.

"Sorry, Colonel," he said. "I reckon I stretched the truth a mite with Lieutenant Harper here."

The colonel came to his feet and glared across the desk at Longarm. "Then who in blazes are you?" he demanded.

"Deputy United States Marshal Custis Long," Longarm said.

And he placed the leather folder containing his badge and bona fides open and facing up on the colonel's desk.

53

Chapter 7

The colonel stared down at the badge and identification papers for a long moment, then lifted his gaze to Longarm again. "You work for Billy Vail?" he asked.

"That's right. You know Marshal Vail?"

A grin cracked the stern expression on the colonel's face. "I was stationed at Fort McKavett down in Texas when a company of Rangers came along on the trail of some Comanches who had stolen a couple of white girls. I took a cavalry patrol out with them, and together we chased down those Comanch' and got the girls back, but not without a sweet little fight on the San Saba River. Billy Vail was the leader of those Rangers."

Longarm returned the grin and said, "I seem to recollect hearing about that fight on the San Saba. Billy said the commander of those cavalry troops was a pretty good fella for a shavetail Army lieutenant."

The colonel threw back his head and laughed. "And considering that those Rangers were only about one step above outlaws themselves, they were a well-disciplined fighting force." He stuck out his hand. "Colonel Ross Thompson. I'm glad to meet you, Marshal Long."

The lieutenant looked a little put out by the scene he

was witnessing. He said indignantly, "Colonel, this man lied to me!"

"Don't get a burr up your butt about it, Harper," Colonel Thompson snapped. "I'm sure the marshal had a good reason for whatever he said. Probably he's doesn't want everyone in the fort to know who he really is and why he's here."

"That's it, all right, Colonel," said Longarm. "I reckon you could say I'm working undercover."

"Why *are* you here?"

Longarm laid the reports on the desk and said, "That'll tell you the story right there."

Thompson motioned Longarm into a chair and sat down again himself as he read through the documents. Lieutenant Harper started to leave the office, but without looking up from the reports Thompson said briskly, "Wait a moment, Lieutenant. You haven't been dismissed."

"Of course, sir," Harper said through gritted teeth.

After a couple of minutes, Thompson handed the reports back to Longarm. "This has the makings of an ugly case, Marshal," he said. "I knew about Miss Davidge and Miss Ralston, of course, but I wasn't aware there were other women missing as well."

Longarm nodded. "You're right about it being ugly, Colonel. Here's the way I've got it figured so far."

He laid out everything he had discovered and everything he suspected concerning the disappearances. Thompson nodded in agreement as Longarm sketched in his theory about how the women had been kidnapped so that their captors could force them into a life of prostitution.

"We're awfully close to the Canadian border," Thompson commented. "But I'm sure you've thought of that already."

"And there's a railroad being built up there," Longarm said with a nod, "which means there are hundreds of men who'd probably be willing to line up and fork over plenty of coin for the chance to spend some time with a young, pretty gal."

"That . . . that's despicable!" Lieutenant Harper burst out.

"Yeah, pretty much," Longarm agreed. "That's why I want you to keep quiet about what you've heard in here this evening, Lieutenant. I've got a feeling those two gents were working on their own, or maybe for somebody across the line in Canada, but it's possible they could still have some spies down here."

"Exactly," Thompson said. "Consider it an order, Lieutenant. You're to say nothing about this matter to anyone. Understand?"

"Of course, sir." Harper had unbent a little while Longarm was talking, and now seemed more like a willing ally.

Thompson turned his attention back to Longarm. "You're going across the border?"

"I don't see what choice I've got. Billy Vail said from the start that I might have to, and he was right. That's why he wired the commissioner of the North West Mounted Police and asked for their cooperation."

Thompson grunted, and Longarm sensed a little disapproval. "The Mounties," Thompson said. "They may look like soldiers in those red uniforms, but they're not. They're more like policemen."

"Might be just the sort of help I need, though, to find those gals . . . and the no-good skunks who carried 'em off."

"Yes, perhaps." Thompson nodded. "Is there anything I can do to help you, Marshal?"

Longarm thought about it for a moment, but then shook his head. "I figure by now there's a good chance those missing women are well across the border. The Army can't go up there without causing a big stink between our government and the Canadians."

Lieutenant Harper began, "But if American citizens have been kidnapped—"

"No, the marshal's right, Lieutenant," Thompson said. "He has permission from the Canadians to cross the border if his investigation warrants it, but an excursion by our military would be nothing but trouble."

"I hope I've got permission," Longarm said. "I ain't heard otherwise from Billy Vail. He knew I was headed in this direction, and chances are he would have sent you a wire asking you to be on the lookout for me and stop me if there was any problem."

"You can use our telegraph line if you want," Thompson suggested. "That way you can get in touch with Marshal Vail before you cross the border."

Longarm considered the idea and then shook his head. "No, I'm just gonna push on with what I've been doing."

The colonel grinned and said, "In other words, if you're not supposed to go into Canada, you don't want to know about it."

Longarm puffed on his cheroot and blew a perfect smoke ring toward a map tacked to the wall of the colonel's office. "I reckon you could say that," he allowed.

Thompson laughed. "Yes, I can see why you work for Billy Vail. The two of you are just alike."

Longarm wouldn't have said that. Vail always worried more about rules and regulations than Longarm did. But maybe back in his Texas Ranger days, when Thompson had known him, Vail hadn't been quite such a stickler for doing things properlike, as long as he got results.

"Do you need supplies?"

Longarm shrugged. "I could use a few provisions, I expect."

"Stock up on anything you want at the trading post, and don't worry about paying for it."

"That's mighty kind of you, Colonel, but I don't figure that'd be a good idea. Might look a little odd if the white slavers do have a spy down here."

Thompson frowned in thought and then nodded. "Yes,

of course, you're right. We can't have anyone thinking that you're getting any special favors. That would make them wonder about who you really are."

"I'm obliged for the thought, though."

"Well, then, if there's nothing we can do . . ."

"Tell me about the gals who disappeared from here," Longarm suggested.

Thompson nodded. "All right. I never saw much of Miss Davidge. She was . . . a mousy little thing, I suppose you could say. A good seamstress, though. She kept our uniforms in good repair."

"What about the missionary lady, Miss Ralston?"

Lieutenant Harper said, "She was very beautiful."

Longarm and Thompson both looked at him in surprise, and a blush spread over his face.

"I, ah, didn't mean to speak out of turn, sir," Harper said to the colonel. "It sort of just . . . came out."

It was pretty obvious to Longarm that Harper had been smitten with Clarissa Ralston. He said, "I've heard she had red hair."

"Yes, indeed," Harper said. "A very striking shade of red. Very attractive."

With a hint of a smile on his weathered face, Thompson said, "Go on, Lieutenant. You obviously paid more attention to the young lady than I did."

"Yes, sir . . . I mean . . . I spoke to Miss Ralston on several occasions. She was quite charming, and very devoted to the Lord's work that brought her here."

"Where did she come from?" Longarm asked.

"Philadelphia, I think."

"She was a Quaker?" The Friends were known for their missionary work on the frontier. Their philosophy of turning the other cheek made them virtually fearless.

"No, I believe she was a Baptist," Harper said.

"Was she in the habit of walking between the fort and the Indian village by herself?"

59

Harper grimaced. "I'm afraid so. I tried to persuade her that she should always have an escort, but she said that the Lord watched over her. I think she believed it would be an insult of sorts if she relied on mere soldiers to protect her."

"Then anybody who spent much time around here wouldn't have any trouble figuring out when the best time would be to grab her."

"I'd say that's a safe assumption," Harper agreed.

"Those men you mentioned," Thompson put in, "they were here for several days, if I remember correctly. Harper, check with the sergeant of the guard about that."

"Yes, sir."

"I couldn't tell you, though, if they left the fort about the same time Miss Ralston and Miss Davidge disappeared," the colonel went on. "I never connected them with the disappearances, so I simply don't know what the timing was."

Longarm nodded. "They seem to have been pretty good about blending into the background and going on about their business without folks paying much attention to them."

"I wish I had paid more attention to them," Harper said. "If I had, Miss Ralston might be safe now, instead of being God knows where, having awful things done to her."

"I'll find her," Longarm said. "I can't change anything that's already happened, but I can sure as hell see to it that the bastards don't get away with it."

Thompson stood up and extended his hand across the desk again. "Good luck, Marshal," he said. "And if you find yourself in more trouble up there than you can handle, get word to us somehow and we'll do what we can to help."

"Even if it causes an international incident?"

"Billy Vail probably never mentioned it," Thompson said, "but during that fight with the Comanches on the San Saba, one of the savages was about to put an arrow right through my gizzard when Billy shot him. He saved my life that day, Marshal, and I never got to repay the favor." Thompson gave a curt nod. "So borders be damned. You need help, you holler and we'll come a-runnin'."

Chapter 8

Longarm left Fort Assiniboine the next morning, dressed in his freshly laundered range clothes and with his saddlebags packed with supplies he had bought at the trading post. He rode north toward the border. Before the day was over, he had crossed the line without knowing for sure that he was in Canada until he came to Ashford's roadhouse and had his encounter with Dooley McCarren and Little Fawn.

By that evening he was approaching the railhead. He heard it and smelled it before he actually came in sight of it. The tang of wood smoke drifted over the prairie, as did the ringing of hammers on steel and the shrill whistle of a locomotive. These plains had a gentle roll to them, so Longarm had to ride to the crest of a long, grassy slope before he could see the end of the track.

To the west, the roadbed had already been graded, a long, raw scar in the earth that stretched as far as Longarm could see. In front of him, ties had already been laid down, but the rails had not yet reached them. That point was still a quarter of a mile to the east, close enough so that Longarm could see the work crews wrestling the five-hundred-pound rails into position and hear the ringing reports as more laborers moved in with their mauls to drive the spikes that fastened the rails to the ties.

Reining his horse to a stop, Longarm looked past the railroad workers to the construction train, which was parked several hundred yards farther east. This train was pushed by a locomotive in its rear, rather than pulled by one in front. The flatcars that made up most of the train were stacked high with steel rails, wooden ties, and all the other supplies necessary for the building of a railroad. Those supplies were loaded onto horse-drawn carts and carried up to the railhead as needed.

Beyond the flatcars were several large boxcars with windows cut into them. Longarm knew that inside those cars were the narrow, cramped bunks where the workers tumbled down exhausted at the end of each day. They were rolling barracks, nothing more.

There were also a pair of windowless boxcars, a mess car where the men ate, and a couple of passenger cars used as offices and living quarters by the men in charge of the construction. Finally, the big Baldwin locomotive with smoke belching softly from its diamond-shaped stack brought up the rear, pointing to the east.

That wasn't the end, though. Beyond the construction train, Longarm saw his real destination.

Hell on Wheels.

Dozens of tents were scattered on both sides of the tracks. Several of them were quite large. Those would be the makeshift saloons, gambling dens, and brothels. All manner of vice was available to the men who were building the Canadian Pacific across whatever province this was. Longarm wasn't sure if it was Saskatchewan or if the railroad had already reached Alberta. It didn't really matter, he supposed. He was still in Canada, one way or the other.

The smaller tents served as the temporary homes of the gamblers, whiskey peddlers, soiled doves, and assorted crooks who followed the railhead. As Longarm heeled his mount into motion and rode toward the tents, he saw to his surprise that some of the inhabitants appeared to be building wooden structures. He wasn't quite sure where they had gotten the boards, since this prairie was treeless for the most part. The lumber must have been hauled in on wagons from somewhere else. Some of the denizens of this place were trying to make it a more permanent settlement.

That wasn't such a bad idea, Longarm reflected. Once it was completed, the Canadian Pacific would need stations spaced out along its length, and chances are those stations would be located in already existing settlements. Down in the States, along the route of the Union Pacific, quite a few of the supposedly temporary towns that had sprung up during its construction had remained in existence once the railhead moved on. North Platte, Julesburg, Cheyenne, Laramie, and many other settlements had gotten their start as Hell on Wheels towns. With a little luck, an ambitious man could get rich in a situation like this.

A ruthless man could get even richer.

Longarm turned his horse so that his route paralleled the tracks on their southern side. As he passed the work crews laying down the rails, he heard something he hadn't expected: singing. After a moment he even recognized the tune. The laborers were singing "Drill, Ye Tarriers Drill!" as they laid down the rails and spiked them into place.

Longarm didn't stop to talk to any of the workers or their bosses. If he was to find what he was looking for, it would be in the burgeoning tent city farther along the rails. He reined his mount to a walk as he reached the crude settlement.

Though it was growing late in the afternoon, the hour was still too early for the big tent saloons to be doing much business. Most of the railroad workers were still at their jobs and wouldn't be free to spend their hard-earned wages until later in the evening.

One enterprising hombre had driven some poles in the

ground to form a square, strung some ropes between them, and called the resulting enclosure a corral. He was sitting on a barrel next to the rope when Longarm rode past, and he called out, "Hey, mister! Better put your horse up here. I'll take good care of him for you, and it won't cost you much."

Longarm reined in and turned the horse toward the makeshift corral. "How much?" he asked.

"Four bits a day."

"American money?"

The man grinned as he stood up from the barrel, revealing himself to be short and bandy-legged. "Sure. American, Canadian, it don't make much difference along the railroad. It all spends."

"You'll see that the horse is fed?"

The man waved a hand at the thick grass inside the corral. "Still plenty of graze right here. If they eat it down too much, I just pick up and move. I give 'em water regular like, though."

Longarm nodded as he swung down from the saddle. He handed the reins to the man and said, "It's a deal. What about my gear?"

"I'll keep an eye on your saddle. Best take your rifle and saddlebags with you, though."

Longarm followed that advice and slid his Winchester from the saddle sheath. He unstrapped the saddlebags and slung them over his shoulder.

"Where does a fella spend the night in this burg?"

"Lots of open prairie if you don't mind sleepin' under the stars," the corral man answered with a gap-toothed grin. "If you want somethin' a mite fancier than that, try the hotel."

Longarm looked around, baffled. "Hotel?"

"Right down yonder." The man pointed to a large tent with a sign hanging over its opening. Sure enough, Longarm saw that the sign read, in crudely printed letters HOTEL.

Longarm left his horse at the corral and walked along what passed for a street in this rudimentary settlement, his eyes taking in all the sights. He passed a tent with a sign on a stake in front of it that read EATS. Another one, obviously owned by somebody with more grandiose ambitions, was dubbed the Maple Leaf Restaurant. He saw a blacksmith laboring at an open-air forge that had the beginnings of some plank walls around it. The smith planned to build his shop around him during his spare moments as he worked. Further along the street, a cobbler sat on a stool in front of a tent and tacked new soles on work shoes. There was the beginning of a real town here, Longarm thought.

The more respectable elements were vastly outnumbered, though. The larger tents had names like the Great North West Saloon, the Saskatchewan Palace, and the Grand Canadian. Smaller ones had signs that read simply WHISKEY, sometimes misspelled badly or scrawled almost illegibly. Longarm passed one sign that proclaimed GUD WOOSKI. Grinning to himself, he hoped that the proprietor brewed better Who-hit-John than he spelled.

He pushed aside a canvas flap and entered the "hotel." A scarred table was set up just inside the entrance. A thickset man with heavy black beard stubble on his cheeks sat there rolling a wet cigar from one corner of his mouth to the other. A shotgun with its stock and both of its barrels sawed off short lay on the table in front of him. He looked up at Longarm and asked, "What can I do you for, eh?"

Longarm looked along the rows of cots set up inside the tent. They were jammed closely together. Some had ratty blankets and thin pillows on them, while others were bare. A few were occupied by men snoring heavily.

"Got a vacant bunk?" Longarm asked.

The man rolled his cigar and nodded. "Take your pick of the ones with no bedding on them. You got to furnish your own bedding."

"All right. How much?"

67

"Dollar a night."

Longarm let out a low whistle. "That's sort of steep, pard."

"Take it or leave it. I'll be full up later."

That was probably true, thought Longarm. There were only a few vacant cots. Still, he said, "It only costs four bits to put up my horse."

"Go sleep with your horse then."

Longarm felt a surge of anger, but didn't show it. He said, "No, thanks, I'll pay the dollar."

"In advance."

"American money all right?"

"It all spends," the man said. Evidently that was sort of a motto around here.

Longarm gave him a five-dollar gold piece. "That'll hold my bunk for a few days, right?"

"Just leave your gear on it. Nobody'll bother it."

Oddly enough, Longarm believed him. In this gathering of gamblers, con men, and crooks, you might get your throat cut and your pockets emptied as you walked along the street at night, but petty theft would be a rarity. Even robbers and murderers had to have someplace they could leave their belongings and be reasonably confident they would still be there when they got back.

Longarm picked out a vacant bunk and laid his rifle and saddlebags on it. None of the nearby cots was occupied at the moment. He went back to the front of the tent and asked the proprietor, "What's the best place to get a drink?"

"The Saskatchewan Palace," the man replied without hesitation. He tongued the cigar to the other side of his mouth. "My brother runs it."

"Much obliged." Longarm considered asking the man about the two hombres he was looking for, but then he decided against it. He wanted to have a look around on his own first, to see if he could spot them, before he revealed his interest in them. He did pause in the tent's entrance, though, and look back at the man. "Has this settlement got a name yet?"

"They call it Bear Paw. Don't ask me why. Probably ain't a bear this side o' the Rockies. Buffalo Shit would be a better name. There's still dried chips layin' all over the prairie."

Longarm went out, grinning and thinking that if frontier settlements were named appropriately, most of them would have "shit" somewhere in their name.

He walked back along the street toward the Saskatchewan Palace. The name of the place pretty much settled the question of which province he was in. With the approach of dusk, some of the railroad workers were now walking from the railhead into the settlement, seeking some relaxation and entertainment after their long day's labor. Saloonkeepers lit lamps hung on poles erected in front of their establishments. The day's work on the railroad was just about over.

The night's work in the saloons and gambling dens of Bear Paw was just beginning.

Chapter 9

Canvas doors at both ends of the Saskatchewan Palace were lifted and tied back, creating a draft through the tent saloon that made the flames in the oil lamps sway and flicker. The breeze carried away some of the tobacco smoke and the stench of unwashed bodies too, and as a result the air was better than it was in most frontier saloons. The hard-packed dirt floor was good about soaking up spilled whiskey, beer, puke, and piss too. Which was not to say that the smell in the place was fragrant, but Longarm had been in plenty of saloons that smelled worse, he thought as he paused just inside the entrance to have a look around.

There were bars on both sides of the tent, crude affairs consisting of broad planks stretched across whiskey barrels. The area in between was packed with tables. Poker games were going on at some of the tables, while at others men sat and drank and fondled the women who carried trays of drinks among them.

As he looked at the women, Longarm couldn't help but wonder if some of the ones he was looking for were right here in front of him. After a moment's thought, he doubted it. None of them looked particularly happy to be serving drinks and being pawed in a tent saloon on the Saskatchewan plains, but they seemed willing enough and didn't have the look of prisoners.

The owner of the place had also freighted in a roulette wheel and a faro table, and both of those games were busy. Toward the back there was an open space where men and women could dance, but at the moment nobody was tripping the light fantastic. Longarm looked through the open flaps at the rear of the tent and saw a dozen smaller tents arranged in a double row with a narrow aisle between them. The area back there was dimly lit by an occasional lantern hung from a post. Those tents were the equivalent of shantytown cribs, he thought. Maybe that was where the missing women were.

That possibility appeared less likely when he saw one of the serving girls leave the saloon and enter a smaller tent with a bearded customer in tow. Evidently the gals who worked at the Saskatchewan Palace did double duty as waitresses and soiled doves.

Still, this was a place to start, and he did so by strolling over to the bar on the right-hand side of the room and finding a vacant space. After a few moments, a bushy-bearded man in a gray wool shirt and a dirty apron wandered over to him and asked over the din, "What's your pleasure, eh?"

"Whiskey," said Longarm.

A grin split the man's tangled beard. "Good, 'cause that's all we got. Well, other than gals, if you want one o' them."

"I'll think on it," Longarm said. "The whiskey first, though."

"Comin' up." The bartender half-filled a glass from a tap stuck directly into the barrel below the bar. "Six bits."

Longarm thought the price was a mite high, but that was typical for a boomtown. He paid for the drink, lifted it to his lips, and threw it back. The rotgut burned all the way down his throat. It was potent, foul stuff.

"Got any with a little less gunpowder and strychnine in it?" he asked as he thumped the empty glass on the bar.

The bearded man laughed. "Sorry. Out here that's the best you're gonna find."

"Well, then, give me another, old son."

As the bartender refilled the glass, he said, "You're an American, ain't you?"

Longarm nodded. "Yeah, just rode up from Montana Territory."

"Lookin' for work on the railroad?"

"No, I've laid my share of track in my life. I thought there might be some other way to earn a little cash up here, though."

"There are plenty of ways," the bartender agreed, "but most of 'em are immoral or illegal or both."

"Well, no job's perfect," Longarm said. That drew another laugh from the bartender.

"No, I reckon not. How are you with cards?"

"Fair to middlin'."

The bartender scrutinized him in the inconstant light of the oil lamps. "You're a pretty big fella. Can you handle that gun on your hip?"

"I'm still alive," Longarm said pointedly.

The bartender drew the correct conclusion from that answer. "Yeah, I thought so. We got plenty of gamblers around here, but what we're short of sometimes are fellas who can keep these tarriers in line when they get rambunctious. Think you could handle that, laddybuck?"

Longarm hadn't come in here looking for job as a bouncer, but since fate had tossed the chance in his lap, it might not be a bad idea to accept it for now. As the biggest saloon in Bear Paw, the Saskatchewan Palace was in the center of everything that was going on. A man who kept his eyes and ears open might be able to learn quite a bit in here.

He sipped the whiskey this time, wanting to keep a clear

73

head, and said, "I can handle whatever you need handled, friend."

The bartender held up his hands, calloused palms out. "Oh, it ain't me who makes the final decision. You got to talk to Queenie."

"Where do I find her?"

The bartender pointed across the room and said, "Right there."

Longarm turned and glanced where the bearded man was pointing, then looked again, longer this time. The woman who stood behind the bar on the other side of the tent wasn't very big, which made her difficult to see through the crowd of men. But when Longarm got a better look, he was impressed.

She was young in years, probably in her twenties, but she carried herself with an air of experience. Soft brown hair was cut short and framed a lovely face. Earrings that sparkled in the light dangled from her ears. The dress she wore left her shoulders and her round, tanned arms bare. When she laughed, as she did when one of the railroad workers in front of the bar said something to her, she was even prettier.

Longarm turned back to the bearded bartender. "The fella down at the hotel told me his brother ran this place. That gal's not anybody's brother. She's not much bigger than a minute either."

"Make no mistake, laddybuck. Clive Drummond may own the Saskatchewan Palace, but it's Queenie who really runs things."

"All right then," Longarm said. "I'll go talk to her."

"Tell her Rufus sent you."

Longarm nodded. "I'll do that."

Leaving his second drink unfinished on the bar, he turned and began making his way across the big tent. It wasn't easy, as busy as the place was. He had to work through crowds of laborers in brogans, dirty canvas trousers, wool shirts, and either derbies or slouch hats. The noise level was an assault on the ears. He began to worry that when he finally reached the other bar, Queenie would no longer be there.

But she was, and he felt her eyes watching him with interest before he even got there. When he finally reached the bar, she had a bottle in her hand. "Drink, stranger?" she asked in a surprisingly musical voice. "This is the prime stuff."

"I thought you only sold one kind of tonsil varnish in here. That's what Rufus said."

"Everything in the barrels is the same," Queenie said with a smile. "This is my private stock."

"Sounds good to me. I'm obliged."

She poured the drink and slid it across the bar. Longarm picked up the glass, being careful not to spill any of the amber liquid as the man on his right jostled him a little. Longarm ignored that and sipped the whiskey, raising his eyebrows in surprise as it went down smoothly. Queenie hadn't exaggerated about the quality.

"What do you think?" she asked.

"Pretty good," Longarm said. "Maybe not as good as Maryland rye, but I doubt if there's a bottle of that within five hundred miles."

Queenie laughed again. "You're probably right about that, cowboy. What's your name?"

"Custis Parker, ma'am."

"Don't ma'am me. My name's Queenie. That's all anybody calls me."

Longarm downed the rest of the whiskey and licked his lips. "All right, Miss Queenie."

"No, just—never mind. A gent as tall and handsome as you, Custis, can call me anything you want. Just don't call me—"

"Late for supper," Longarm finished for her.

"My God, you're a man after my own heart! Let me refill that glass for you."

Longarm put his hand over the top of the glass. "No, thanks. It's mighty good, but I don't like to get addlepated before I start talking business."

Instantly, Queenie was wary. "Are we about to talk business, Custis? If we are, I have to tell you . . . I don't work the tents out back."

Longarm shook his head and said, "Not that kind of business. Rufus over on the other side of the tent told me you might be looking for somebody to keep trouble from breaking out in here. If you are, I'm your man."

"I like the sound of that last part," she said, evidently flirting with him out of habit. "And we could use another head-knocker to keep these railroad men in line. Rufus is big enough to handle some of that, and so are the other bartenders, but I'd like to have somebody circulating through the tent, ready to jump in right away if a fracas breaks out."

"I'm looking for work, and I'll do a good job for you."

"I believe you would," she said. "But there's one test you've got to pass first." She reached across the bar and touched his hand. "Come with me."

Longarm wasn't sure where she was going to take him or what sort of test she had in mind, but he figured he would play along for now. Queenie came out from behind the bar and took his hand, leading him toward the front of the saloon.

"I have a tent of my own not far from here," she said, quietly enough so that only he could hear her in the hubbub around them. "It's a lot nicer than the ones out back."

"You lead the way, Queenie," Longarm murmured.

Before they could reach the front of the tent, however, several men bulled into the saloon. Queenie stopped short and muttered, "Hell."

"Trouble?"

"Could be. That's Eamon Kelly and his friends. They're usually looking for a fight."

Longarm didn't have much doubt which of the men was

76

Kelly. That would be the tall, burly one with the blue-black beard stubble on his pugnacious jaw and the troublemaking look in his eyes. He was dressed like a railroad worker, but he had put on a corduroy jacket over his wool shirt and brushed up the derby on his head. Obviously he was ready for a night on the town—if Bear Paw could be called a town.

The three men with him were big and tough-looking too, but Kelly was clearly the leader. He stopped just inside the entrance and looked around, and his eyes lit up when he saw Queenie.

"Hello, darlin'," he greeted her in a booming voice. "I was hopin' to run into you."

"Well, you can just get over that hope, Eamon," she told him briskly. "I was just leaving."

Kelly's grin disappeared, turning into a glare as he looked at Longarm. "With this ugly spalpeen?"

"No call to be insulting, friend," drawled Longarm. "We don't even know each other."

"And I don't want to know ye," Kelly said. "All I'm after is spendin' some time with Queenie here."

"I told you," Queenie said tautly, "that you're welcome to drink and gamble here, and if one of the other girls wants to go with you, that's fine. But I don't do that."

Still looking at her, Kelly reached out and poked Longarm hard in the chest. "Then why are ye leavin' with this scut?"

"Mr. Parker and I have some business to discuss."

"Business?" Kelly snorted. "Whore business, you mean!"

"That's enough," Longarm said. "Step aside and let us be on our way, Kelly."

The Irishman sneered at him. "Or what?"

Longarm wondered if he had actually heard right. This was rapidly turning into the sort of confrontation kids had in schoolyards. At least, he'd had a few such run-ins during his limited educational career back in West-by-God Virginia before the war. But he was a grown man now, not a snot-nosed youngster, and he didn't need this kind of shit.

He took Queenie's arm and started to steer her around Kelly and the other toughs. "Come on," he said quietly. He expected Kelly to give him a shove and cuss him, but maybe it wouldn't go that far.

Kelly didn't bother with any more preliminaries, however. Instead, he hauled off and swung a malletlike fist straight at Longarm's head, as fast and hard as he could.

The blow might have taken Longarm's head off if it had connected, but it wasn't fast enough. Longarm moved to the side and let the punch go harmlessly past his ear. Kelly stumbled against him, thrown off balance by missing with the blow. Longarm let go of Queenie's arm and hooked a short punch to Kelly's midsection. His fist traveled about six inches, but it landed with such force that it was buried almost to the wrist in the man's belly. Kelly's florid face turned pale as he gasped in surprise and pain.

"I warned you, old son," Longarm muttered.

Kelly stumbled back a step, clutching himself. His mouth opened and closed as he tried unsuccessfully to form words. The men with him moved forward, evidently as surprised as Kelly himself to see their leader stricken helpless like that. But they were angry too, and when Kelly finally got his voice back and choked out, "Get the bastard!" they lunged at Longarm with fists swinging.

So far, this was an isolated incident near the entrance to the saloon. If it turned into an all-out brawl, though, it would likely engulf the whole place, and there was no telling how much damage might be done before it was over. This was just the sort of thing that Longarm was supposed to prevent if he got that job.

So he moved fast, almost too fast for the eye to follow as he kicked the first man in the crotch, palmed out the Colt on his left hip, reversed the gun, slammed the butt across the face of the second man, and then flipped the revolver around again so that the third man found himself staring into its barrel at short range. The man stopped short, trembling with the effort to halt the punch he'd been trying to throw. His eyes widened as he looked at the Colt, and his tongue came out of his mouth to lick nervously over his suddenly dry lips.

"Back up, old son," Longarm said quietly. "No need for this to go any further."

"Yeah . . . Don't shoot, eh?" The man started to move back.

Kelly wasn't ready to give up, though. He had caught his breath, and suddenly, with a roared curse, he snatched up a chair and swung it at Longarm. The chair crashed down on the big lawman's arm and forced it toward the ground. Queenie scrambled out of the way as Kelly lunged at Longarm, tackling him around the waist.

Longarm went down hard, bumping several people as he fell. Men shouted curses and questions and got out of the way. Longarm was pinned to the ground by Kelly's considerable weight. The Irishman tossed the chair aside and snatched a knife from his belt. He raised his arm. The blade was poised to drive down into Longarm's chest.

It looked, Longarm thought, like he was going to have to shoot the son of a bitch.

But before the blade could fall, a strong, bronzed hand shot out of the crowd and closed around Kelly's wrist. The corded fingers twisted hard and sharp, and there was a snapping sound. Kelly gave a thin scream of pain as the knife slipped from suddenly nerveless fingers and fell harmlessly to the ground.

The man who had broken Kelly's wrist released it and ducked back into the crowd, disappearing almost in the blink of an eye. Longarm shoved the groaning Kelly aside and surged to his feet, checking to see that Kelly's companions were still out of the fight. The one he had kicked in the balls was curled up on the ground, as was the man he had walloped with the Colt. The fourth bully had decided on the better part of valor and gotten the hell out of the Saskatchewan Palace.

Longarm swung around to look for the man who had helped him, but there was no sign of him. Longarm's eyes narrowed as he thought about the brief glimpse he had gotten of the man's face.

Then Queenie clutched his arm and asked anxiously, "Are you all right, Custis?"

"Yeah, I'm fine as frog's hair," Longarm replied. "I just wish those varmints had listened to reason and not started such a ruckus."

Queenie laughed. "You call that a ruckus? That was nothing. That chair Kelly hit you with didn't even break. And those other two you put down never knew what hit them." She motioned for Rufus and one of the other bartenders to drag Kelly and his remaining two friends out of the tent. Then she linked her arm with Longarm's and said, "Come on. We still have to have that discussion."

"Sure," he said, but as they left the tent saloon, his mind wasn't completely on what Queenie might have in store for him. He was thinking as well about the man who had broken Kelly's wrist.

The ragged clothes had been the same, and so had the scruffy beard and the grimy face.

The question was, why had a man that strong and fast and dangerous pretended to be a drunk and let those sergeants down at Fort Assiniboine push him around like they had?

Chapter 10

Queenie didn't disappoint him. As soon as they were in her private tent, she moved into his arms and tilted her face up so that he could kiss her. She was so short that Longarm had to bend over a considerable amount to reach her lips with his, but the kiss was well worth the effort. Her mouth was hot and wet and sweet, and she thrust her tongue between his lips with a hungry urgency.

Longarm slid a hand down her back to the gentle swell of her rump. She was slender but possessed all the soft, enticing curves that were necessary. Her breasts were like two small, firm apples against his chest as she molded her body to his.

She slipped a hand between them and pressed her palm against the hardness at his groin, rubbing it with a rotating motion that made his shaft swell even more than it already had. After a moment her fingers went to the buttons of his trousers. Deftly, she unfastened them and reached inside to free his manhood from confines that had grown too tight.

His pole sprang loose, jutting out proudly from the opening in his trousers. Queenie took hold of it with both small hands, and gasped against Longarm's mouth when she was unable to close her fingers around its circumference. She broke the kiss and looked down in awe as she stroked her hands from the base to the tip of his shaft.

"My God, you're so big around!" she said in a hushed tone. "And so long! It'll never all fit inside me, Custis."

"Does that mean you don't want to try and see for sure?" he asked.

She gave her delightful laugh. "No, that's not what I mean at all. Wild horses couldn't drag you away from me now."

Still holding his stiff member with both hands, she leaned over and began to lick it, running her tongue around the head. She squeezed hard and milked a drop of moisture from the slit at the tip and lapped that up. Longarm closed his eyes as pleasure washed through him at what she was doing. She opened her mouth and took the head of his shaft inside, but that was all she could get past her lips. Her tongue quivered and fluttered against the crown as she sucked him, stimulating him to the point that he was about to loose his seed down her throat. With practiced skill, she pulled back at the last moment, leaving him awash in sensation.

"Now me," she said urgently as she lay back on the bed and pulled her skirts up.

It was a real bed too, not a cot. This was a good-sized tent, with room not only for the bed but also a table and a couple of ladder-backed chairs. A sturdy wooden chest with iron straps and a latch sat at the foot of the bed. A thick, woven rug had been laid down on the hard-packed ground. The lamp burning low on the table filled the room with a soft yellow glow.

That glow revealed the inviting, sparsely furred mound between Queenie's thighs and glistened on the damp folds of the opening just below it. She spread her stocking-clad legs wide in invitation. Longarm dropped to a knee beside the bed and leaned forward to accept the invite. His big hand reached between her thighs and covered her entire core. She moaned softly as she thrust her pelvis against his palm. He massaged her slowly, tenderly.

She was already breathing hard when he used his thumbs to spread her open even more, leaned over, and speared his tongue into her wet, heated center. That penetration was enough to send her over the edge. Her hips bucked up off the mattress and her thighs clamped around Longarm's head. Dew flooded her. He kept licking and sucking as her climax rolled through her in a series of delicious shudders.

After a long moment of ecstasy, her legs fell apart loosely, freeing his head and allowing him to rise up again. Her chest rose and fell rapidly. Her eyes were closed and her face wore an expression of joy.

She didn't stay that way for long, though. She rolled over, got her hands and knees underneath her, and thrust her rump in the air. "Take me," she murmured to Longarm. "Take me from behind."

Longarm was always glad to oblige a lady, especially when she asked him so nice. Both of them were still dressed, but neither wanted to take the time to strip off their clothes. Besides, the important parts were uncovered. Longarm stood at the edge of the bed, grasped Queenie's hips, and brought the head of his shaft to her fevered opening. With a steady surge of his hips, he thrust into her, sliding between those slick lips and sheathing himself inside her.

At first he thought she had been right that he wasn't going to be able to get all of his organ in her. She was incredibly tight as well as hot. Firmly, he held onto her and pushed harder. She pulled a pillow over to her and buried her face in it to muffle her cries of pleasure as he spread her open more and more. Finally, he had delved as far into her as he could go. His shaft swelled and throbbed, and just that movement against her sensitive inner walls was enough to send her into a shuddering climax once more.

Longarm held himself in place and let the ripples subside. When Queenie finally let out a long sigh of content-ment and her muscles relaxed, he began a slow stroking in and out of her. He withdrew almost all the way and then leisurely eased his way in again. Like stoking a fire, he gradually built up her excitement. At one point, she gasped, "Custis, I . . . I don't know how much more I can take!"

"You can take it all," Longarm told her.

"Yes!" she cried softly. "Give me all you've got, Custis!"

He complied, steadily thrusting harder and harder and increasing the speed at the same time. Queenie rotated her hips against him and then bucked back hard with them be-fore returning to the rotation. After a few minutes, though, she was too carried away for anything fancy. She just thrust back against him, meeting his driving strokes into her. Her core was drenched. She whispered, "Yes, yes!"

Longarm felt his climax boiling up. Holding tightly to her hips, he plunged into her one final time and then stayed there, buried as deeply within her as he could go, as his culmination washed over him and he surrendered to it. His shaft swelled and grew even thicker as his seed gushed from him. He emptied himself into her in spurt after shud-dering spurt. She spasmed against him as he filled her to overflowing.

This time they were both sated, and when Queenie started to slump down onto the bed, Longarm didn't try to stop her. His shaft slid wetly out of her. She lay on her belly, trying to catch her breath. Longarm was a mite limp-legged himself, so he sat on the edge of the bed and rested a hand in the small of her back. Queenie made a little sound of pleasure in her throat and moved her hips slightly as he caressed her.

When Longarm's thundering pulse had slowed a mite, he said, "Was that the test you wanted me to pass before you hired me?"

Queenie lifted her head and looked around at him in confusion. "What? . . . Oh, you mean what I said back there in the saloon." She laughed. "Forget about that, Custis. I was just joshing with you."

He frowned. "You mean you ain't gonna hire me?"

"Not at all. I'd decided to hire you before we ever left the bar. And I knew I was right when I saw the way you handled Eamon Kelly and his friends. What happened here was just because the moment I saw you, I knew I wanted to feel you inside me."

Longarm leaned over and kissed the small of her back where he had been massaging her. She gave a purr of contentment.

As nice an experience as this had been, he couldn't forget that he had come to Bear Paw on business. And now he had yet another mystery to solve, he reminded himself. He said, "Did you happen to get a look at the fella who gave me a hand in that ruckus?"

"What?" She looked back over her shoulder at him. "What are you talking about, Custis?"

"When Kelly was about to take a knife to me, somebody reached out of the crowd and grabbed his wrist. Twisted it so hard that he broke it, in fact. I was just wondering who the hombre was."

Queenie shook her head. "I didn't see him. I thought you did something to Kelly to disarm him. It all happened so fast, it was confusing."

"Fights usually are," Longarm said. "This gent looked to be just a little shorter than me, so he was pretty good-sized. Dressed in old clothes, had dirt on his face and a little beard. Was wearing an old slouch hat, I think."

"You've just described a few hundred of the men around the railhead, Custis. I'm afraid I don't have any idea who you're talking about."

"Well, I reckon it's not really important," he said with a shrug. "Just some Good Samaritan, I suppose."

But he didn't really believe that for a minute. It was too much of a coincidence that the mysterious stranger had shown up here in Bear Paw after literally running into Longarm at Fort Assiniboine. Had the man followed him up here, or had Longarm inadvertently followed the stranger?

Longarm didn't know the answer to that question, but he swore to himself that the next time he bumped into the fella, he was going to find out.

In the meantime, there was still the matter of the missing women from the States. He said, "With this many men around, they must be pestering you all the time, as pretty as you are."

"Those railroaders don't care what a girl looks like, as long as she's female. But I make it clear pretty quick that I'm not a whore." Queenie twisted around and reached up to rest her hand on Longarm's cheek. "When I do this, it's because I want to, not because I'm getting paid to do it."

"But you've got whores working for you," Longarm said.

"Well, of course." She frowned slightly. "You're not one of those sanctimonious fellows who thinks there's something wrong with that, are you, Custis?"

"Not hardly. I was just wondering where you come up with gals to work for you. There's not a whole lot of folks out in this part of the country."

"Well, that's true enough," she said with a pretty shrug. "But most of the working girls don't come from out here. They're from back East, and they've been at it for a while. They've followed the railroad all the way from Ontario."

Longarm nodded. "Makes sense. You must lose some of them along the way, though. A gal gets sick or in the family way, or she marries one of her customers, or she decides to just up and leave. . . ."

"Why all the questions? Are you interested in becoming a whoremonger, Custis?"

Longarm held his hands up in surrender. "Nope, just curious. I'm bad about that. I see something that interests me, and I start asking all sorts of questions."

"Well, there's nothing much more simple than prostitution. The woman has something a man wants, and the man is willing to pay for it. And you're right: Some of the girls leave, and it can be difficult to replace them, especially out here on the prairie, in the middle of nowhere. But we manage."

"I'm sure you do."

Queenie sat up and started unbuttoning her dress. "Let's get these clothes off," she suggested. "I want to be naked with you until you're ready to go again."

That sounded like a fine idea to Longarm. He shucked his duds in a hurry, and within minutes he and Queenie were naked together on the bed, cuddling against each other. His shaft started to thicken again. She reached down and curled one hand around it, as far as she could reach anyway.

"Have any other questions?" she asked with a mischievous grin on her face.

"As a matter of fact . . . I was wondering if maybe you'd seen a couple of fellas I know who might be up here. They were headed in this direction the last time I heard anything about them."

She propped herself up on an elbow and stared down at him. "You're serious?" She gave his shaft a squeeze. "You'd rather talk right now?"

Longarm took hold of her hips and rolled onto his back, lifting her bodily so that she was poised above his erect member. She braced her knees on either side of him and lowered herself onto him, taking him into her gradually, sliding down his pole until it was fully lodged inside her. Then she began to rock her hips back and forth. It was a delicious sensation, but Longarm didn't give himself over to it completely. He said, "It wouldn't take but a minute to tell you what they look like."

She collapsed on his broad chest, shaking with laughter. "Oh, all right," she said. "Go ahead."

"One's a big fella, bigger even than me."

"Bigger . . ." She thrust her hips a time or two. "Down there, you mean?"

"I, ah, wouldn't know about that."

"I don't see how anybody could be bigger than you, Custis, but go ahead."

"He wears a . . . buffalo coat." The things she was doing were beginning to get to him. "And his pard is only . . . about half his size . . . and wears a derby."

"I don't . . . wait a minute." She gasped and moved her hips faster. "My God! . . . I don't think I've . . . seen them . . . Oh, Custis!"

He cupped her breasts and thumbed her hard nipples. She rode him at a gallop, and in seconds she began to shudder as a fresh climax gripped her. Longarm surged up into her and spurted again.

When they were finished, Queenie lay on his chest and rested her head on his shoulder. "Like I was saying," she murmured, "I don't think I've seen them, but I'll ask around if you want."

"That'll be fine." He stroked her bare, quivering flanks. "I appreciate it."

"Not as much as I appreciate what you've done for me tonight, Custis."

He held her close and said, "The feeling's mutual, darlin'."

Chapter 11

What with one thing and another, they didn't make it back to the Saskatchewan Palace that night. Nor did Longarm have to sleep on the narrow cot in the so-called hotel.

He woke up early the next morning. Queenie lay next to him, her back to him so that they were snuggled together spoon-fashion. She appeared to be sound asleep. Longarm hated to move. Few things were more pleasant than waking up with a beautiful naked woman in your arms, he thought.

But he had work to do, and he wasn't going to accomplish anything by cuddling with Queenie, no matter how much fun it was, or how warm and soft she was, or . . .

He put those thoughts out of his mind and eased away from her before his manhood got so hard that it started poking her in the rump. All he needed was for her to wake up and push back against him, and then, before you knew it, they'd be all hot and bothered again and he wouldn't get out of there for an hour or more.

He hoped Billy Vail knew just what sort of sacrifices he made in the name of his job. Then he decided that maybe he hoped Billy *didn't* know.

Longarm managed to get out of the bed without waking Queenie, though she sighed in her sleep as if she missed the warmth of his body pressed to hers. He pulled his clothes on and went to the tent's entrance, where the canvas flap was tied tightly closed. Not so tightly that some sunlight didn't penetrate around it, however.

He untied the flap and slipped out quickly and quietly, closing it behind him and hoping the light hadn't disturbed Queenie. Bear Paw's main street was almost deserted this early. All the railroad workers had gone back to their boxcar barracks the night before, and the saloon folks were still asleep.

Slipping a cheroot out of his shirt pocket, Longarm lit it and starting looking for someplace he could get some breakfast. He picked the place with the EATS sign out front, figuring it would be less pretentious than the Maple Leaf Restaurant. When it came to breakfast, simpler was usually better.

The smell of coffee that wafted to his nose as he pushed through the tent's entrance flap told him that he had made the right choice. It was a good smell, rich and bracing.

Inside he found a long table with benches on each side. At the far end of the tent was another table loaded down with food. Customers would move along that table and fill tin plates, then pay the proprietor and claim a cup of coffee at the end before finding a place to sit at the main table. At the moment that wouldn't be a problem, because only half a dozen men were seated there, happily putting away piles of flapjacks and bacon. Longarm looked past them at the man running the place, who was bald as an egg and had curling black mustaches. He was short and broad and his muscles bulged against his shirt. Not the sort that anyone would guess to be a cook, but that was one of the good things about the frontier: You couldn't tell everything about folks just by looking at them.

Longarm started past the table toward the food, but he stopped short as he glanced at one of the customers sitting alone at one end of the table. The man met his gaze squarely at first; then his eyes darted toward the entrance flap as if he was thinking about making a run for it. Then, obviously, he changed his mind. He looked levelly at Longarm again for a second and then went back to eating.

He was a cool-nerved son of a bitch, Longarm had to give him that. But Longarm's nerves didn't get rattled easily either. The big lawman went on to the front table, loaded a tin plate with food, and carried it over to the proprietor.

"That will be four bits," the man said in a French accent, reminding Longarm that there were a lot of folks of French descent in Canada. Enough so that some of them thought they ought to have a part of the country for their own. Some years back a fella named Louis Riel had caused a ruckus over that very thing.

Longarm paid for the food, took the cup of coffee the French-Canadian handed him, and went over to the table. He sat down deliberately next to the man he had noticed earlier. "Morning," he said pleasantly.

"Good morning," the man replied. His voice had a powerful tone to it, not at all the sort of voice you'd expect from a down-at-heels tramp. But despite his appearance, he obviously wasn't a tramp.

Longarm ate in silence for a couple of minutes, washing down the flapjacks and bacon with sips of strong black coffee that tasted as good as it smelled. Finally he said, "I'm obliged for the hand you gave me last night."

"I don't know what you're talking about."

"In the Saskatchewan Palace," Longarm said. "When Eamon Kelly was about to stab me and you broke his wrist. I don't reckon you saved my life or anything, since I still had my Colt and I would've shot the bastard before I let him stick that blade in me, but I'm grateful I didn't have to."

The man glanced at the other customers, who were gathered at the other end of the table, talking among themselves, apparently not paying any attention to the low-voiced conversation between Longarm and this mysterious stranger. After a moment, he said, "Think nothing of it. I just didn't want to see anyone get hurt."

"Kelly yelled like it hurt when you broke his wrist."

"I got . . . carried away."

Longarm took a swig of coffee, chewed a bite of food, and swallowed. "Just like those sergeants down at Fort Assiniboine got carried away when they tossed you out of the trading post because you were nothing but a stinking drunk. Only thing is, you weren't drunk at all, were you? You let them hoo-raw you."

"Listen," the man hissed. "I don't know what you're talking about. I've never been to Fort Assiniboine."

"You and me both know different, old son."

The man put down his fork and gave a sigh of frustration. In a half whisper that only Longarm could hear, he said, "Would you like it, Marshal, if I began telling all and sundry who you really are?"

Longarm stiffened. So this hombre knew he was a lawman. That didn't come as a complete surprise. But as the man guessed—correctly—Longarm didn't want that news spread all over Bear Paw.

"We need to find us a place where we can talk in private," he suggested.

"Yes, under the circumstances, that seems like a good idea. I have a camp a short distance north of here, out of sight of the railhead. I'll meet you there in, say, half an hour?"

"How far north? Will I need my horse?"

"Yes. Ride about a mile due north. You'll see some brush to your right. There's a gully just beyond the brush. I'll be waiting for you there."

Longarm nodded. "All right. I'll be there."

The man sighed as he looked down at his plate. "I knew I shouldn't have given in to my craving for bacon," he muttered, as much to himself as to Longarm.

92

He finished his meal a minute later and stood up to leave, dumping his empty plate and cup in a wash barrel as he walked out of the tent. Longarm took his time about finishing his own breakfast. When he was done, he said to the owner, "That was mighty good grub, old son."

The French-Canadian nodded solemnly and said, *"Merci, monsieur."*

Longarm left and headed for the tent hotel, where he picked up his Winchester. The man who had been there the day before was nowhere in sight. Longarm walked on down to the makeshift corral. When he got there, the man who ran it grinned at him and said, "I hear you're workin' for Clive Drummond and Queenie at the Palace."

"Word gets around fast in this place, don't it?"

"I keep my ear to the ground," the man said sagely. "You want your horse?"

"Yeah, I thought I'd take a ride and keep the critter's legs limbered up. Get a little fresh air too, away from the smoke of that locomotive."

The day's work was already under way on the railroad. The construction train's locomotive was getting steam up. Before the day was over it would push the cars farther west along the tracks.

Longarm saddled up and rode across the tracks. He pointed the horse north.

It was possible he was riding into a trap, and he knew it. The stranger knew he was a lawman and might want to get him out of the way. But if that was the case, Longarm mused, why hadn't the man just let Eamon Kelly stab him the night before? Longarm had helped out the stranger down at Fort Assinniboine, pulling him out of the mud when he'd landed in it face-first, but Longarm was convinced now that the man hadn't really been drunk. He wouldn't have let himself choke to death. So Longarm hadn't saved his life any more than he had saved Longarm's. Any way you looked at it, they were even.

93

Which meant that now maybe the hombre intended to bushwhack him. He could try, Longarm thought with a tight grin, but that didn't mean he would be successful.

And when Longarm turned the tables, then he would get some answers.

His eyes never stopped moving, scanning the prairie ahead of him and to the sides as he rode, alert for any signs of an ambush. On these open, rolling plains, it was going to be difficult for anybody to get close to him without being spotted. Longarm was careful anyway. Being cautious was a good way for somebody in his line of work to stay alive.

He saw the brush that the stranger had mentioned long before he reached it. As he rode closer, he watched for the reflection of the sun off a rifle barrel. There was nothing to indicate that he was riding into trouble, though. The plains appeared deserted.

Skirting the brush, he saw the sudden dip in the terrain. At some time in the past, a creek had run through here, carving out a gully, but it was dry now. Longarm reined his horse to a halt and drew the Winchester from the saddle scabbard before he dismounted.

A call came from the bottom of the gully. "Don't worry, Marshal. I'm not going to ambush you. Come on down, please."

The bank was gentle enough along here for Longarm to walk down it easily. He turned to the right and followed the gully, which made a sharp bend after only a few yards. He went around the turn with the Winchester in his hands ready to fire.

He saw that the gully narrowed here and the banks were steeper. Somebody could ride past fifty yards away and never know this place was here. The ashy remains of a small fire lay close against the bank on one side of the gully. A good-looking, saddled black horse was tied to a hardy bush that grew out of the side of the gully.

The stranger stood there with a mirror in his left hand and

a razor in his right, scraping the beard off his jaw. He had scrubbed his face clean too, and discarded the ragged old clothes. Now he wore high-topped black boots and brown trousers over a suit of long underwear. The suspenders attached to the trousers were down while he shaved.

He finished with the razor, ran his fingers over his jaw searching for any stubble he had missed, and evidently found none because he cleaned the razor in a small basin of water, folded it, and slipped it into a pack that hung from his horse's saddle. "That feels much better," he said as he pulled his suspenders up.

Longarm already had a pretty strong suspicion who, or at least what, this gent was. He lowered the Winchester and said, "I reckon you're gonna take a red coat out of that pack next, aren't you?"

The stranger smiled. "Indeed. Quite perceptive of you, Marshal Long." He reached into the pack, pulled out the short red coat Longarm had alluded to, and pulled it on. He buttoned up the brass buttons, buckled a wide black belt around his waist, and then stepped over to Longarm and held out his hand. "I suppose formal introductions are in order. I'm very pleased to meet you, Marshal. I'm Constable John Ryerson, North West Mounted Police."

Chapter 12

"So you're a Mountie," Longarm said as he shook John Ryerson's hand.

The Canadian lawman frowned slightly. "I'm a constable in the North West Mounted Police. The term *Mountie* is not necessarily offensive, but it's a bit informal."

"So's dressing in ragged clothes and pretending to be a drunk," Longarm pointed out.

Constable Ryerson shrugged. "I thought it best to keep my true identity a secret, especially since I was conducting an investigation outside of my legal jurisdiction."

Longarm took out a cheroot and put it in his mouth. "Yeah, about that," he said. "I thought you boys were sticklers for rules and regulations, but there you were down in Montana Territory, pretending to be something you ain't."

"As were you," Ryerson pointed out.

"Yeah, but I'm a deputy U.S. marshal, and last I checked, Montana was still part of the United States."

Ryerson spread his hands. "Guilty as charged. What more can I say? Except that when I heard about how those women and girls have been disappearing, I wanted to get to the bottom of it as badly as you apparently do, Marshal."

Longarm frowned and said, "I figured you must know

about that." He struck a lucifer on his thumb and set fire to the gasper clenched between his teeth.

"Indeed," said Ryerson. "I was in this area when I received word from Inspector Steele that an American peace officer might be entering Canadian territory in the course of an investigation and that I was to render whatever aid you might request, as long as it was in my power to do so. The message also contained a concise summary of the case to which you were directing your attentions."

"So after you heard all that," Longarm said, "you took it on yourself to cross the border and do a little undercover work of your own."

Ryerson stiffened his back and squared his shoulders. "A North West Mounted Policeman is trained to use his own initiative as required."

Longarm could understand that. The actual number of Mounties out here in the Canadian West was fairly small, and the area they were responsible for keeping law and order in was vast. They wouldn't have the time to clear every move with their boss before they took action.

Sort of like deputy U.S. marshals, Longarm thought with a wry grin that he concealed by lifting his hand to take the cheroot out of his mouth.

"All right, at least our cards are on the table now," he said. "What's our next move?"

"You think we should work together then?"

"Not too close, no." Longarm gestured toward the distinctive red coat Ryerson wore. "You ride back into Bear Paw wearing that and inside an hour everybody up and down the rail line will know that you're a Mountie. I don't plan on announcing just yet that I pack a badge."

"Perhaps not, but I think that we should still share whatever information we've uncovered on the case. As a gesture of good faith, I'll go first." Ryerson took a deep breath. "I believe those women and girls were kidnapped so that they could be brought up here and forced into a life of prostitution."

"Yeah, by a couple of fellas driving a closed-up wagon. Big one in a buffalo coat and a little hombre in a derby."

It was Ryerson's turn now to frown in surprise. "Yes, that's my theory as well."

"We've been dogging each other's trail, old son. And it's led us to Bear Paw."

"Out here, the railroad workers are the only source of potential income for anyone running such a prostitution scheme," Ryerson said. "The missing women *must* be somewhere around the railhead."

Longarm nodded. "But they're not working at the Saskatchewan Palace. That's the only thing I'm pretty sure of so far."

"How do you know that?"

"Because *I'm* working at the Saskatchewan Palace, as a bouncer."

"Indeed! When did this come about?"

Longarm put the cheroot back in his mouth and said around it, "Got hired on there last night."

"By the woman called Queenie? Or by Clive Drummond?"

"My dealings were with Queenie," Longarm said. "I haven't even seen Drummond yet. Talked to his brother at the hotel, though."

"Yes, Frederick Drummond. They're an ugly pair. I suspect they were involved in criminal activities back East before they came out here to the plains."

"The hotel seems to be run on the up and up. From what I've seen so far, so is the saloon. They've got soiled doves working for them, all right, but the gals ain't prisoners and don't seem upset about being there. Can't arrest the Drummond brothers for that."

"Prostitution *is* illegal, you know."

Longarm waved a hand. "You arrest all the whores and put them out of business, the railroad workers will strike . . . that is, if they don't have themselves an old-fashioned riot. I reckon it's more important to the Canadian government to get that railroad finished than it is to clean up the morals of the fellas building it."

"You're correct about that," Ryerson admitted. "However, Inspector Steele has received permission to enforce the laws in a five-mile strip along both sides of the railroad right-of-way. Once the ban is in place, no liquor, gambling, or prostitution will be allowed in that zone."

Longarm let out a low whistle. "You'll have your hands full enforcing that, Constable."

"Undoubtedly, but enforce it we shall."

"When does the ban go into effect?"

Ryerson shook his head. "I don't know yet. Inspector Steele is supposed to be sending some more men out here so we can be ready when the new policy is announced."

"Ready for trouble, you mean."

"Ready for whatever comes," the constable said.

"Well, that's your worry, not mine. I'm just up here to find those missing gals."

"Working at the Saskatchewan Palace should be a good place to start. You'll hear a great deal of gossip there. Perhaps in time you'll hear something that will lead you to the men you're after."

"Only one problem with that," Longarm said. "I ain't got a lot of time. There's no telling what all has been happening to those gals, but it's pretty damned certain it's been bad, and it's just gonna get worse for them."

"Yes, that's true, of course." Ryerson frowned in thought for a moment, but then his expression cleared as an idea obviously occurred to him. "What you need, Marshal, is a way to force the miscreants you seek out into the open."

"I was thinking along the same lines," Longarm said.

"Although I got to admit I never really thought of 'em as miscreants. More like low-down bastards."

"Yes, they're that too. I can help with this dilemma. I'll ride into Bear Paw in my uniform, as if I've just arrived in the area, and announce that I'm looking for those two men. I can ask questions about them all over town."

Seeing where Ryerson was going with this, Longarm said, "If you do that, word will get back to them and they're liable to start gunning for you."

Ryerson grinned broadly. "Of course! That's exactly the plan. And this red coat of mine will make me quite a fine target, don't you think?"

Longarm had to admit that it would. "So when they come after you, I go after them."

"Exactly." Ryerson extended a hand. "What do you say, Marshal? Do we proceed with this plan?"

"You'll be running a mighty big risk," Longarm pointed out.

"Nonsense. I have faith in you, Marshal."

Longarm hoped that faith wasn't misplaced. He couldn't think of a better idea, though, so he took Ryerson's hand and said, "You've got yourself a deal, Constable."

Longarm returned to Bear Paw first. Ryerson planned to wait until later in the day, then circle back to the east and approach the railhead from that direction. As Longarm rode toward the Hell on Wheels settlement, he thought about the plan he and Ryerson had worked out. If he'd had his druthers, he would have preferred to be wearing the target on his back. Since Ryerson was a Mountie, though, Longarm had to admit that the constable was the logical choice to be the one that flushed out the men they were after.

It wasn't yet midday when Longarm reached Bear Paw. Work on the railroad was in full swing. The chuffing of the locomotive, the ringing of hammers on spikes, and the raucous songs of the laborers drifted over the prairie. Longarm had heard that cacophonous racket many times. It was the sound of progress, and like it or not, there was no stopping it.

The settlement still had a sleepy air about it, although more people were up and about now than there had been earlier when Longarm rode out. All the saloons, gambling dens, and cribs wouldn't get lively, though, until late in the afternoon when the railroad workers began to drift back in this direction. The folks who ran all those establishments were in for an unwelcome surprise sometime in the near future, when the Mounted Police forced them to move at least five miles away from the tracks. But until that happened, plenty of money would still change hands in those illicit enterprises.

He put his horse up at the rope corral and then walked along the street to the Saskatchewan Palace. The entrance flaps were down but untied. Longarm pushed one of them back and went inside.

Only a few of the lamps were lit at this time of day, leaving much of the room inside the big tent in gloom. One of the lamps hung over the bar to the left, however, and Queenie stood at that bar, wearing a plain brown dress now instead of the gaudy, provocative getup of the night before. Standing next to her was a chunky man with very black hair and a pouchy, bulldoglike face. Longarm guessed he was Clive Drummond.

That hunch was confirmed a moment later when Queenie glanced at him and then said to the man with her, "There's Mr. Parker now, Clive."

Drummond grunted. "Well, bring him over here. I'd like to meet him."

Queenie motioned for Longarm to come over to the bar. Longarm went, but took his time about it. Even though he was pretending to be working for her, he didn't want her thinking that he was completely at her beck and call.

Besides, her tone of voice had been rather cool, and she

102

continued that as she said, "Good morning, Mr. Parker. I trust you slept well."

So that was the way she wanted to play it, he thought. There was probably something going on between her and Drummond, and she didn't want him thinking that she had spent the night with Longarm. Of course, plenty of people had seen him leave the Saskatchewan Palace with her the night before. Drummond was bound to hear about that and draw his own conclusions sooner or later.

For now, though, Longarm played along with Queenie and touched a finger to the brim of his Stetson as he nodded to her. "Yes, ma'am," he said. "I slept just fine. Like a baby, in fact."

Drummond said, "I hear Queenie hired you to help keep the peace in here."

"That's right. Reckon that makes me a peace officer of sorts."

"Don't even joke about that," Drummond snapped. "There's no law out here yet, and that's just the way we like it."

"Me too," said Longarm.

"I hear you busted up Eamon Kelly and his bully boys pretty good."

"You hear a lot of things, don't you, Mr. Drummond?"

"It pays to keep an ear to the ground. What about Kelly?"

Longarm shrugged. "He's the one who decided to fight, not me. But if a fella comes at me, it ain't my habit to back down."

"Good. Keep that attitude. You'll need it with those bull-necked railroaders. They're a hotheaded bunch, and they love to fight."

"They can fight all they want," Longarm said, "just not in here."

Drummond nodded and extended his hand. "Good. I reckon you'll do, Parker."

Longarm shook hands with the saloon owner and said, "I'll do my best."

Drummond smiled faintly. "I trust Queenie to run this place for me, but never trust anybody too much, especially a woman. Right, Parker?"

Longarm saw the glance that Queenie directed at Drummond behind the man's back. It wasn't very friendly.

"I reckon you're right, Mr. Drummond." That got Longarm a look too, but one that wasn't as hostile. Evidently Queenie understood that Longarm was just playing along with Drummond.

"It won't get busy for a good while yet," Drummond went on. "Be back here by late afternoon. Until then, you're free to do whatever you want."

"I'm going to go out back and check on the stock in the storage tent," Queenie put in. Longarm wondered if that was a hint for him to meet her back there. Seemed to him it would be taking a chance, what with Drummond being so close by. Maybe Queenie was one of those gals who enjoyed a touch of danger.

Longarm lit a cheroot, lingering there until Queenie was gone. Then he said to Drummond, "Since I've got some time to kill, what's the best place around here for an hombre to find a willing gal?"

"The girls who work here will accommodate you," Drummond said. "Just don't abuse the privilege."

Longarm rolled the cheroot in his fingers. "Well, no offense, Mr. Drummond, but I was sort of wondering about some younger, fresher gals. Most of those waiter girls you got have been around the block a time or two."

"Or more," Drummond agreed. He regarded Longarm intently from narrow, deep-set eyes. "Like 'em young, do you?"

"Not too young," Longarm said. "Sixteen or seventeen maybe." Several of the missing girls had been that age. Even though he had worked out the plan with Constable

Ryerson, Longarm wasn't going to stop trying to find out things on his own.

"All right," Drummond said. "It might be that I know where you can find what you're looking for."

Longarm waited for him to go on, but before Drummond could say anything else, sunlight flashed as somebody pushed in through the entrance flaps. Longarm glanced over his shoulder and stiffened, recognizing the newcomer as Eamon Kelly. Kelly's broken right wrist was splinted and wrapped up with bandages. So he used his left hand to raise the heavy revolver he pointed at Longarm as he shouted, "Now, you bastard, you're mine!"

Chapter 13

Longarm's instincts took over as his hand flashed across his body to the Colt in the cross-draw rig on his left hip. Even with his speed, though, he couldn't outdraw an already drawn gun. The revolver in Kelly's left hand boomed as flame spurted from its barrel.

Longarm heard the wind-rip of the slug past his ear as he fired from the hip. His bullet caught Kelly in the body and knocked the hate-crazed railroader back a step. Kelly managed to stay on his feet and fired again. But the barrel of his gun had dropped as his strength rapidly deserted him, and the shot thudded into the hard-packed ground in front of Longarm.

Kelly let out a groan as he tried to lift the gun for a third shot. "Give it up, old son!" Longarm called to him. "You're hit bad already, but you might live through it."

Kelly ignored the warning, grated a curse, and continued struggling to bring the gun to bear. Longarm muttered a curse of his own and squeezed off another shot. The slug drove deep into Kelly's chest and flung him backward so that he fell through the entrance flaps and landed half in and half out of the tent.

From behind Longarm, Queenie screamed, "Oh, my God!"

For a second Longarm thought she was worried about him, but then a glance over his shoulder showed him that Clive Drummond was down. The saloon owner lay on his back, gasping as he pawed feebly with one hand at his bloody chest. Kelly's first shot, the one that had whipped past Longarm's ear, had found Drummond instead.

Queenie rushed to Drummond's side from the rear entrance of the saloon and dropped to her knees beside the wounded man. Knowing that he couldn't do anything for Drummond that Queenie couldn't do, Longarm strode over to Kelly's sprawled form. Kelly had dropped the revolver when he fell. Longarm kicked it farther out of reach, then pushed the canvas flap back so that he could get a better look at Kelly's face. The Irishman's blue eyes stared up sightlessly. He was dead as he could be.

Drummond might still be alive, though. Longarm wheeled around and went back to the bar. He heard Drummond's raspy breathing. The man's eyes were closed. He had passed out, but he wasn't dead yet.

"Is there a doctor around here?"

Queenie didn't respond to the question, so Longarm asked it again, louder and sharper this time. Finally, she looked up at him, her face pale and shocked, and said, "The . . . the railroad has a doctor for the workers. I don't know if he'll help us."

"He'll help us," Longarm replied grimly. "If he's a real sawbones, he swore an oath that says he has to."

With that, Longarm holstered his gun and swung around. His long strides carried him quickly out of the tent and over to the railroad tracks. He walked along them until he passed the locomotive and came to the two passenger cars. That was probably where he would find the construction superintendent.

He clattered up the steps at the front of the first car and

opened the door without knocking. Several men were gathered around a table inside, studying some topographic maps that were spread out on it. They looked up in surprise, and one of the men snapped, "Who are you? What are you doing in here, mister? This is private property."

"Looking for the doc," Longarm answered. "A man's been shot."

"I thought I heard some shooting a few minutes ago." The man frowned. "Where did this affair take place?"

"In the Saskatchewan Palace."

The man turned away dismissively. "Not our problem, then. Our doctor treats only railroad employees."

A couple of strides brought Longarm to the table. His hand came down heavily on the man's shoulder. "Damn it, you'd better point me to the sawbones now." He hadn't particularly liked Clive Drummond, but Drummond had been hit when Kelly was shooting at Longarm and the big lawman felt like he ought to do something about it. It wasn't his fault—Kelly had pulled the trigger, not him—but still, Longarm wasn't going to just stand by and allow Drummond to die.

Of course, it might be too late already. . . .

"Get your hands off me," the railroad man said coldly. "Do you know who I am?"

He was medium height, with a dark mustache and a pointed smudge of a beard. Longarm had never seen him before.

"No, I don't, and I don't care. Just tell me where to find the doctor and I'll get out of here."

One of the other men said, "Why don't you just tell him, Rossley? That would be the easiest way to get rid of him."

"I'm Clarence Rossley," the man glaring at Longarm said. "The construction superintendent."

"I don't much care if you're Queen Victoria's favorite nephew," said Longarm. "There's a man bad wounded who needs help."

Rossley shrugged off Longarm's hand and said angrily, "Oh, all right. Come on."

He led Longarm to the next car, where a thin, sandy-haired man sat with a thick book open in his lap.

"Dr. Davis, this man requires medical attention," Rossley said.

The sawbones looked Longarm over through thick spectacles. "You don't seem to be wounded," he said.

"That's because it's somebody else who got ventilated. Come on, Doc. Time's a-wastin'."

Davis grabbed a black medical bag and followed Longarm out of the car. They walked quickly toward the tent town. Davis's legs were as long as the marshal's, so he didn't have any trouble keeping up.

When they entered the Saskatchewan Palace, Longarm saw that Clive Drummond had been lifted onto the bar. Quite a crowd was gathered around him, including Queenie, Rufus the bartender, several of the girls who worked in the Palace, and some of the other citizens of Bear Paw such as the corral owner and the little mustachioed French-Canadian who ran the place where Longarm had eaten breakfast. Drummond's brother Frederick, from the tent hotel, was there too, looking worried.

"Let us through," Longarm rumbled. "Got the doc here."

The crowd parted, giving Longarm a good look at Drummond. The saloon owner was ashen but still alive, his chest rising and falling in a ragged rhythm. Longarm heard the whistling sound of a punctured lung. So did Dr. Davis. The medico immediately stuck a finger into the bullet hole in Drummond's chest. Drummond's breathing eased somewhat.

"Will he live, Doc?" Queenie asked.

"It's much too soon to say about that," Davis replied. "He's badly wounded, I can tell you that. I'll have to perform surgery, and it might as well be here as anyplace else.

110

Someone hang a lamp right over us, so that I can see properly. I'll need clean clothes and hot water, lots of hot water. And whiskey."

"Plenty of that close at hand," one of the townies said. "Plan on gettin' drunk, Doc?"

"No, I plan on saving this man's life if I can," Davis answered testily. "Now move back, all of you, and give me some room."

Longarm spread his arms and forced the crowd back, all except for Queenie and the doctor. Rufus, who was a pretty big man himself, helped in clearing the space. One of the other bartenders went off to boil water, while one of the women who worked in the Palace said, "I was just doin' some laundry. I'll rip up a clean petticoat and bring it to you, Doc. Will that do?"

Davis nodded. "That'll be fine, thank you. Hurry, please."

He settled down to the work of trying to save Clive Drummond's life. Meanwhile, Frederick Drummond came over to Longarm and demanded angrily, "What happened here? How did my brother get shot?"

Grimly, Longarm replied, "I hate to say it, but the gent who plugged him was aiming at me. Probably would've hit me too, if he hadn't had to use his left hand. That wasn't his shooting hand."

"You're talking about Eamon Kelly?" Frederick snapped.

Longarm nodded. "That's right."

"The man you got in a fight with last night. The man whose wrist you broke."

Actually, it had been Constable John Ryerson, in his disguise as a drunken tramp, who had broken Kelly's wrist, but Longarm didn't explain all that. He just shrugged and said, "Something like that."

"So if not for you, poor Clive wouldn't be lying there right now with a bullet in his chest."

Longarm's face hardened even more. "Kelly pulled the trigger, not me. Nobody forced him to come in here and throw down on me. That was his own choice. What happened to your brother was just pure-dee bad luck."

Frederick grunted and repeated, "Bad luck. Sure. I want you out of my hotel, mister."

"Fine. I'll be by later to pick up my gear."

"See that you do that." Frederick moved over closer to the bar where Dr. Davis was laboring over the wounded Clive Drummond.

In a low, rumbling voice, Rufus said to Longarm, "That don't hardly seem fair. You and the boss was both just standin' there when Kelly came in yellin' like a madman and wavin' that gun around. You put him down as quick as you could. Mighty quick, in fact. I haven't seen a draw quite that slick in a long time." Rufus regarded Longarm shrewdly. "You sure your name is Parker and not Doc Holliday or something like that?"

"I've met Doc," said Longarm. "There's a slight resemblance, but he's shorter than me and a damn sight skinnier. I'm not some notorious shootist, if that's what you're asking. And Parker is my real name." Just not the last name, he added silently.

Rufus shrugged. "No offense meant, friend. I was just curious."

Longarm glanced toward the bar. "Wish I'd been slick enough on the draw to keep Kelly from getting that first shot off."

"Nobody's that fast," Rufus said. "There was nothing you could do."

Longarm believed that. But it didn't make him feel much better.

Dr. Davis worked for a couple of hours over Clive Drummond, opening his chest cavity, removing the bullet, and then sewing up his lung so that it inflated again. When

Davis had cleaned everything up and patched Drummond's chest as best he could, he stepped back, his hands smeared with a thick coating of blood, and shook his head.

"That's all I can do. If nothing festers, this man has a chance. A slim chance, to be sure, but better than nothing, I suppose."

Queenie's face was pale and drawn, but she nodded and said, "Thanks, Doc. He'd be dead by now if it wasn't for you."

"I suspect you're right."

Queenie looked at Drummond and asked, "Is he going to wake up?"

"Probably not for a long while, perhaps days or even weeks, if he lives that long. He may never regain consciousness. On the other hand, he may wake up five minutes from now. You never know. That's highly unlikely, though."

Longarm overheard the conversation and damned the luck. He was glad that Drummond was still alive, but as long as the saloon owner was unconscious, he couldn't answer any more questions. Longarm remembered bitterly that Drummond had been about to tell him where he could find some young prostitutes when Kelly had come in and ruined everything.

He'd just have to find those women some other way, Longarm told himself.

There was nothing he could do here. He slipped out of the Saskatchewan Palace and walked over to the hotel tent. Frederick Drummond wasn't there. A balding, middle-aged gent Longarm hadn't seen before was sitting behind the table that served as a registration desk. He nodded as Longarm said, "I'm just picking up my possibles. Won't be staying here any longer."

"We're sorry to see you go, friend," the balding man said, not sounding like he meant a word of it. Longarm suspected he didn't.

The Winchester was still on his saddled horse. Longarm picked up his saddlebags from the cot he hadn't gotten around to using. As he turned to leave, he said to the clerk, "I paid for five nights."

"You want a refund, you'll have to take that up with Frederick Drummond. I ain't authorized to give out any money, only to take it in."

Longarm had figured as much. He nodded and left the place.

As he stepped out of the hotel tent, he heard a commotion from the street. Looking toward the east, he saw that a rider on a big black horse had just entered Bear Paw from that direction, following the railroad tracks. The hombre was drawing a lot of attention from the people on the street. His jacket was a bright scarlet in the afternoon son.

Constable John Ryerson of the North West Mounted Police had arrived.

Chapter 14

"A Mountie!"

"By God, it's a Mountie!"

"Mountie's come to town!"

The shouted comments from the bystanders floated to Longarm's ears. He saw that Constable Ryerson was ignoring the shouts, especially the ribald gibes about how pretty he looked in his bright red jacket. He wore a stiff campaign hat set exactly squarely on his head, and he kept his eyes trained rigidly in front of him. He rode through the settlement and went to the work train, no doubt intending to speak first to Rossley, the construction superintendent.

Ryerson never even glanced at Longarm, but the big lawman had the feeling that the constable had spotted him anyway.

Since he and the Mounted Policeman weren't supposed to know each other, Longarm watched Ryerson ride by with the same amount of curiosity shown by the other citizens of Bear Paw, no more and no less. When Ryerson had dismounted and gone into the first passenger car behind the locomotive, Longarm slung his saddlebags over his shoulder and walked toward the Saskatchewan Palace.

Before he got there, a small procession emerged from

the tent saloon. Queenie and Dr. Davis led the way, followed by Rufus and several other men carrying a makeshift litter on which Clive Drummond lay. Drummond was still unconscious and pale as death, though his bandaged chest rose and fell slowly.

Longarm met the group and asked, "Where are you taking him?"

"To my tent," Queenie replied. "I've got the best bed in the whole settlement—"

That wasn't telling him anything he didn't already know, thought Longarm.

"—and Clive will need a good place to get a lot of rest, where somebody can look after him all the time," Queenie. went on. She looked down at Drummond with what seemed to Longarm like genuine affection. Clearly, Queenie didn't mind bedding other men, and she didn't agree with everything Drummond said and did, but she still felt something for him anyway. Other than the romping on the side, it reminded Longarm a little of an old married couple, and he suddenly wondered if maybe Drummond and Queenie really were hitched, or at least had been together for long enough that they might as well have been.

"Who's going to run the saloon?" Longarm asked as he walked along with the group toward Queenie's tent.

"I'm sure Frederick thinks he is," she replied, and he heard the dislike in her voice when she mentioned Drummond's brother. "I intend to keep an eye on it myself, as much as possible, and Rufus is trustworthy too." She looked up intently at Longarm. "Can I trust you, Custis? You've been in Bear Paw less than twenty-four hours, you know."

"You can trust me," Longarm said. "I got no designs on taking over your saloon, you can sure believe that."

After a second, Queenie nodded. "I do. Thanks, Custis."

They had reached their destination. Carefully, the men carried Drummond into the tent and transferred him to the

116

bed under the doctor's supervision. Davis checked Drummond's pulse and listened to his breathing. "Not too bad," the sawbones declared. "I'll be back to check on him when I can. My first duty is to the Canadian Pacific, though."

"I'll make it worth your while to take good care of him, Doc," Queenie said.

"Like I said, I'll do what I can . . . or what Clarence Rossley will allow me to do."

Mention of Rossley made Longarm wonder how the conversation had gone between the construction superintendent and Constable Ryerson. He and Ryerson would have to work out some system of meeting clandestinely, so they could continue to exchange information.

Since Frederick Drummond had kicked him out of the hotel, and since he couldn't stay with Queenie, he was going to have to find someplace else to hang his hat, Longarm mused. He slipped out of Queenie's tent and starting walking idly around the settlement. As a matter of habit, though, he kept his eyes open. A fella never knew when he might see something interesting.

When it got to be midday, Longarm's stomach reminded him to eat. He went back to the French-Canadian's tent and found that the food was just as good as it had been at breakfast. After he had finished off a large bowl of stew, Longarm stopped to chat for a moment with the proprietor.

"You wouldn't happen to know of a good place around here for a fella to stay, would you, old son?"

"There is the hotel run by M'sieu Frederick Drummond."

Longarm shook his head. "Nope, I've been booted out of there."

"Because of the gunfight that left M'sieu Drummond's brother wounded?"

"That's right."

"But that was not your fault," the man said. "You were attacked."

Longarm shrugged. "That don't make ol' Frederick any more hospitable."

"You have a bedroll, *m'sieu*?"

"Yeah, I do."

The French-Canadian made an eloquent gesture toward the tent surrounding them. "I sleep here at night. I would be happy to share it with you, *m'sieu,* for no charge. Put two of those benches together and spread a bedroll on top of them, and it makes an adequate bed. Nothing fancy, you know, but not too bad."

Longarm rubbed his chin as he thought. "I do believe I'll take you up on that. I'm Custis Parker."

"Claude Renoir."

"Like that French painter fella," Longarm said. They shook hands. "Pleased to meet you, Claude. Reckon I could leave my saddlebags with you while I'm not here."

"But of course. Where are you going, Custis?"

"Well, I've got to be at the Saskatchewan Palace a little later. I'm working there, and just because Drummond got shot, it don't mean things won't be business as usual at the saloon. Until then, I thought I'd just walk around town some more and see what there is to see in Bear Paw." Longarm lowered his voice to a conspiratorial tone. "To tell you the truth, I'm in the market for a little female companionship, if you get my drift."

"*Oui, certainment.* But I have no suggestions for you along those lines."

"That's all right. I'll root around and see what I can find."

Longarm left the eatery and spent the afternoon dropping into several saloons, nursing a drink for a while in each one. He dropped hints to the bartenders, but the only women they steered him toward were all older and more experienced in the game.

He had just stepped out of one of the tent saloons when he saw Ryerson striding toward him. Longarm kept all signs of recognition off his face as the scarlet-jacketed Mountie came up to him and said, "Good afternoon, sir. Constable John Ryerson of the North West Mounted Police. Perhaps you'd allow me to ask you a question?"

"Why, I reckon that'd be all right," Longarm replied.

"I'm looking for two men. Perhaps you know them, or have seen them." Ryerson described the big man in the buffalo coat and the little one in the derby hat.

Longarm shook his head. "No, I don't recollect seeing anybody who looks like that. Why are you looking for them, Constable?"

"It's an official matter," Ryerson said vaguely. He touched the brim of his hat politely. "Thank you for your cooperation."

The constable moved on down the street, leaving Longarm to look curiously after him for a moment. Then Longarm shrugged and walked on in the other direction.

It was all an act, of course, but there had been several people on the street nearby, and if they had overheard the conversation, as they likely had, they would believe that Longarm and Ryerson had never met before now. Their plan called for Ryerson to ask all over the settlement about the two men they were looking for, so it might have looked a little odd if he had neglected to question Longarm.

He hoped Ryerson had more luck than *he'd* had so far. Longarm hadn't seen any sign of the missing women or the men who had kidnapped them. That one comment Clive Drummond had made just before he was shot was the only shred of a lead Longarm had so far, and as long as Drummond was unconscious, that didn't do him any good.

Or did it? Maybe whatever Clive Drummond knew, his brother knew as well. Of course, Frederick didn't have a very high opinion of Longarm and likely wouldn't be very cooperative. Longarm started giving some thought to how he might approach the man and try to find out what he wanted to know.

In the meantime, there was still his job at the Saskatchewan Palace. If he kept his eyes and ears open, as he intended to, there was no telling what he might find out there. It was late enough in the day so that the saloons were starting to get busy. Longarm headed for the Palace.

When he came in, Rufus raised a hand at the bar, summoning him over. Longarm nodded to the burly, bearded bartender, and asked him, "Have you heard how Mr. Drummond's doing?"

"Same as before," Rufus replied. "He's alive, but just barely."

"Hasn't woke up yet?"

Rufus shook his shaggy head. "Nope. Queenie was here a little while ago, figuring out which of the girls was gonna sit with Drummond tonight."

Longarm frowned and said, "She's not staying with him herself?"

"No, she feels like she's got to be here." Rufus leaned forward over the bar and lowered his voice. "I think she had a run-in with Frederick Drummond this afternoon. Those two don't like each other, and I reckon they don't trust each other either."

That was the impression Longarm had gotten too.

"You want a drink?" Rufus asked.

"No, I'm working now. Better keep a clear head."

"Probably a good idea. Say, have you heard about that Mountie bein' in town?"

"Yeah. In fact, I talked to him this afternoon. Seems like he's on the trail of a couple of fellas."

Rufus nodded. "He was in here a while ago, askin' questions. I don't know who those gents are or what they might've done, but I wouldn't want the Mounties after me. They're a stubborn bunch. They don't give up when they're tryin' to track down a fella, from what I hear."

Longarm nodded. He didn't think Rufus was lying. The bartender didn't know the two men he and Ryerson were after. That was good to know, because he liked Rufus. He would have hated to think that the bartender was part of the plan to kidnap American women and force them into prostitution.

One of the women who worked in the Palace moved behind Longarm, carrying a tray of drinks, and he took advantage of the opening to incline his head toward her and ask Rufus, "Where do all these gals come from? They been working for Drummond for a long time?"

Rufus wiped the bar with a rag as he answered, "Yeah, they came with him from a saloon he had back in Winnipeg. For that matter, so did I."

Longarm nodded. He had suspected as much from everything he'd seen. In fact, if he had been less confident in his hunch, he might have started to wonder if he was wrong about the missing women being around Bear Paw at all. He certainly hadn't seen any sign of them.

And yet they had to have gone somewhere. Everything his investigation had turned up down in Montana Territory pointed to Canada. Bear Paw was the nearest outpost of civilization, and with all the railroad workers around here, it fit in perfectly with the theory that both Longarm and Constable Ryerson had arrived at independently.

So where were those blasted missing gals?

Queenie came in a few minutes later, when Longarm was no closer to an answer than he had been. As she took off the shawl draped around her shoulders, he saw that she had changed from the conservative brown dress she had worn earlier into a more low-cut gown that exposed the rounded swells of the upper half of her breasts. She was lovely, despite the strain Longarm could see on her face.

She walked over to the bar and nodded to Longarm and Rufus. "Is everything going all right?" she asked.

"Yeah, you don't have to worry, Queenie," Rufus assured her. "Business is good, and there ain't been no trouble."

Queenie looked at Longarm. "What about those friends

of Kelly's who were with him last night? Do you think they'll come back looking for revenge like he did?"

Before Longarm could answer, Rufus said, "I doubt it. They must've heard how Custis here gunned down Kelly without a lick of trouble."

"What about it?" Queenie asked the big lawman.

Longarm shrugged. "Those boys struck me as followers. With Kelly gone, I don't think they're likely to cause a problem."

"I hope not. Come with me out back, Custis."

The command was sharp enough so that Longarm would have been annoyed if he hadn't been pretending to be a loyal employee. As it was, he shrugged again and said, "Sure."

They left through the tent saloon's rear entrance. Queenie led him past the small tents where the working girls did this part of their business to a somewhat larger tent. She pulled the flap back to reveal a couple of dozen barrels of whiskey stored inside the tent. They went inside and Queenie let the flap fall shut behind them.

It was shadowy inside the tent, but Longarm didn't need to see very well to know that Queenie was suddenly in his arms, pressing her body urgently against his. Her arms went around his neck and pulled his head down to hers. Her mouth found his in a hot, searching kiss.

Longarm certainly didn't mind kissing a delectable little morsel like Queenie, but he thought her behavior was a mite strange considering how upset she had been earlier about Clive Drummond being wounded. He put his arms around her waist anyway and held her tightly. When she finally broke the kiss, she rested her head against his chest and shuddered.

"Thank God you're here, Custis," she murmured. "I know I haven't known you for long, but you're about the most man I've met in ages."

Longarm hated to ruin the moment, but he wanted to make sure what was going on here. He said, "It sure ain't that I'm opposed to kissing you, Queenie, but I thought you were all broken up about what happened to your boss."

"You mean Clive?" She lifted her head to look up at him, even though neither of them could see very well in the gloom. "Of course I'm upset and worried about him. But that doesn't mean I don't still have other feelings."

"You two have a sort of understanding then . . . ?"

"An understanding?" She suddenly clapped a hand over her mouth and said, "Oh, my God. You think that Clive and I are lovers?"

"Well, I don't know. . . ."

"Custis, Clive Drummond is my father. Frederick is my uncle."

Longarm frowned. That news was a bigger surprise than he liked to admit. He'd had no idea that Drummond and Queenie were father and daughter.

"He's your pa, and he lets you work in a saloon?"

She laughed softly. "Clive learned a long time ago not to try to keep me from doing anything I really want to do. As you put it, we have an understanding . . . just not the sort that you meant." She reached up and put a hand behind Longarm's neck. "So you don't have to feel guilty when we do this."

She kissed him again.

Folks dealt with stresses and strains in different ways, Longarm told himself. Clearly, Queenie believed in relieving some of her tension through physical means.

So when she slid down to her knees in front of him, undid the buttons of his trousers, brought out his rapidly hardening shaft, and took it in her mouth, he didn't try to stop her.

Hell, he told himself, he probably couldn't have anyway, even though she was a little bitty thing.

She continued sucking him with great skill for several minutes, but when Longarm felt his climax approaching, she must have too, because she stopped and stood up quickly, saying, "Set me on one of those barrels."

Longarm put his hands around her slender waist and lifted her with no trouble to the top of a whiskey barrel. She pulled up her gown, spread her legs, and cocked her hips so that the opening to her wet core was lined up with Longarm's erect manhood. He moved between her legs, brought the head of his shaft to the slick, heated lips of her femininity, and thrust inside her. Queenie wrapped her legs around his hips and pulled him even deeper within her. She put her arms around his neck and held on tightly as he drove in and out of her in a fast, intense rhythm. Neither of them were in any mood for delay.

Longarm did pause long enough, however, to say in a rough whisper, "Sometime we ought to try this again with our clothes off instead of on."

"Just keep doing . . . what you're doing . . . Custis," Queenie gasped between teeth clenched in passion.

Longarm launched back into it. Queenie was hot and wet and tight, and it wasn't long before Longarm was ready again. When she began to shudder and spasm against him, he knew that she was too, so he let himself go. He lunged into her and held himself there, buried deeply within her, as his seed flooded out of him in a white-hot tide. Queenie pressed her face against his chest to muffle her scream of culmination.

When Longarm finally ceased jerking and spurting, he kept his arms around Queenie for a long moment. She seemed so limp and satiated in his embrace, he was worried that if he let her go she would topple right off the barrel. Finally, they both got their breath, and he slid out of her and moved a step back, even though he kept his hands on her shoulders.

"Thank you, Custis," she whispered. "I can't tell you

how much I needed that. There's just one more thing I need from you."

"What's that?" Longarm asked.

"I want you to kill my Uncle Frederick," she said.

Chapter 15

Longarm's hands tightened on her shoulders. "What did you say?"

"I want you to kill my Uncle Frederick," she repeated. "I know you can do it."

"Why?"

"Because if you don't, he's going to take the saloon away from me." Queenie's voice broke a little as she went on, "I . . . I know that Clive isn't going to make it. The doctor came by again to check on him a little while ago. He wouldn't say it, but he just shook his head. I'll be surprised if Clive lives until morning."

"And you figure once he's gone, your uncle will move in and take over."

"I know he will," Queenie said. "They've always been partners. Frederick will think it's his right to claim the saloon. Besides, it's very difficult legally for women to own property."

"Way out here, I wouldn't think that whether something is legal or not means very much," Longarm pointed out.

"Maybe not, but civilization is coming to these plains, Custis. That's what the railroad means. Things will change, and Frederick will take advantage of the law to get what he wants . . . unless he's dead."

"You got any other family?"

"No, just my father and Frederick."

"So if both of them were gone, nobody would be able to take the saloon from you."

"That's right." Queenie reached down and rubbed her hand over Longarm's groin. Her voice was husky as she asked, "You'll help me, won't you, Custis?"

"I'm not a hired gun," he said roughly. "I don't kill folks for money."

"I'd certainly be willing to pay you, but that's not really what I'm asking. We can run the Saskatchewan Palace together. Bear Paw will be a real town, an important town. When more ranchers move into the area and there's a railroad station here, there'll be plenty of business. We can get rich . . . together. Think about it, Custis."

He sensed that an outright refusal would turn her against him, and he didn't want that right now. So he frowned and said, "I will think about it. But that's all I can promise you right now."

"All right, but don't take too long about deciding," she said with a sharp edge to her voice. "If you won't help me, there are other men who will. Rufus has always been sweet on me."

Longarm didn't doubt it. He didn't want to see the friendly bartender get drawn into Queenie's murder plot either. He said, "Give me tonight to think it over. I'll let you know tomorrow."

"Let's hope that's not too late." She reached under her dress and adjusted her garments, then slid off the barrel and landed lithely on the ground. "We'd better get back inside." Her hand touched his arm, and her voice softened for a moment. "Thank you, Custis."

"Don't think nothing of it," he told her.

They left the storage tent and went back into the saloon. Longarm rolled one of the whiskey barrels in front of him, a convenient excuse for their trip out back. The place was getting busier, with railroad men lined up at both bars and most of the tables occupied as well. Longarm circulated through the room, alert for trouble, doing his job as a bouncer while at the same time listening intently to the conversations of the men in case anyone dropped a hint that might help him in his real job as a deputy marshal on the trail of a dozen missing women.

Later in the evening, Constable Ryerson came into the saloon. The sight of his scarlet jacket made the conversation suddenly go hushed. Ryerson looked around, spoke briefly to Rufus and the other bartenders, and drifted through the tent, continuing his questioning of the men. Eventually he made his way to Longarm and looked at the big lawman with recognition on his face.

"I spoke to you earlier today, didn't I?" Ryerson asked.

"You sure did, Constable, and I don't know a thing now that I didn't know then." That wasn't strictly true—his discovery of the relationship between Queenie and Clive Drummond had come later, but it didn't have anything to do with the case that Ryerson was investigating.

"Well, then, I don't suppose I need to ask you any more questions, do I?"

Longarm shook his head. "I reckon not."

"If you're going to be like that about it . . ." Ryerson said, raising his voice slightly. He put a hand on Longarm's shoulder. "Come along with me."

"What the hell!" exclaimed Longarm. "You're arresting me?"

"I'm taking you in for further questioning. I don't like your attitude, sir."

"I don't care much for yours either." Longarm knocked Ryerson's hand off his shoulder.

The constable put his hand on the butt of the gun holstered at his waist. "You'll either come along peacefully, or I'll be forced to subdue you."

Queenie appeared at Longarm's side, drawn by the tense confrontation. "Custis, what is it?" she asked anxiously.

"Aw, this redcoat wants me to come with him so he can ask me some more questions I can't answer," Longarm said in a tone of evident disgust.

"We don't need any trouble with the Mounties," Queenie said in a low voice.

"I know. That's why I'm gonna go with him." To Ryerson, he said, "Take it easy, old son. You don't need that gun."

"Come along then," Ryerson said.

With a surly look on his face, Longarm accompanied the constable out of the tent. He felt plenty of eyes on them as the customers watched them leave. Everybody in here would believe that Longarm had gone with Ryerson under duress.

"Not bad," Longarm said quietly when they were out of earshot of the saloon. "Nobody's gonna think we're working together now."

"That was the idea," Ryerson agreed. "Have you uncovered any more information?"

"Not a blasted thing. As far as I can tell, those women ain't in Bear Paw or anywhere hereabouts."

"They have to be. Otherwise we're left in a quandary."

"Wouldn't be the first time I was in one of those varmints," Longarm said dryly. "Usually if I keep shaking the tree, though, sooner or later something falls out."

Ryerson sighed. "That's my hope as well. Perhaps we should make arrangements to meet somewhere tomorrow, away from the settlement. This ruse of questioning you worked well enough tonight, but we can't repeat it."

Longarm agreed, and they quickly worked out a plan to rendezvous at the gully where Ryerson's camp had been around noon on the following day. Longarm turned to go back toward the Saskatchewan Palace, while Ryerson went the other way.

Longarm hadn't taken a dozen steps when a gun blasted somewhere behind him.

He whirled around, his hand going to the Colt in the cross-draw rig. He was in time to hear another shot and to see Colt flame bloom in the thick shadows between a couple of tents. A few yards away, Constable Ryerson was down on one knee. He lifted his gun, took deliberate aim, and fired.

Longarm broke into a run, trying to circle some of the tents and get behind the bushwhacker. Now that Ryerson was returning the hidden gunman's shots, Longarm figured the bushwhacker would cut and run. A Colt blasted a couple of more times in the night, but Longarm couldn't tell if it was Ryerson's weapon or the would-be killer's.

Gravel grated under Longarm's boots as he reached the Canadian Pacific's roadbed. Faint light from the moon and stars showed him a shadowy form running across the tracks. Longarm bounded up the slight incline to the rails and ran across too, angling toward the fleeing man. The gent must have heard someone coming after him, because he suddenly pivoted toward Longarm and triggered a couple of shots. Longarm heard one of the bullets sizzle past his ear. The other slug hit the tracks behind him and whined off in a ricochet.

Aiming at the muzzle flashes, Longarm snapped two shots at the ambusher. The man grunted and went down hard, but he sprang up again and kept moving, limping badly now. Longarm went after him, rapidly closing the gap between them. He could have stopped, drawn a bead, and probably dropped the bushwhacker, but he wanted the man alive so that he could answer questions.

They darted between and around tents. Longarm lost ground when a man came blundering out of one of the

tents, drawn by the shooting. Longarm caromed off the un-
lucky hombre, knocking him ass over teakettle and almost
falling down himself. By the time Longarm caught his balance, he couldn't see the man he was after anymore.

Where was Ryerson? Had the Mountie been hit by one
of those first shots, and if so, how badly was he hurt? Longarm didn't know the answers to any of those questions. He
was literally in the dark, working his way through the tent
settlement on this side of the tracks, watching for any sign
of his quarry.

The bushwhacker could have gone to ground and might
be waiting for him, ready to gun him as soon as he got a
chance. That was a risk Longarm had to take. The plan he
and Ryerson had hatched had worked, and fairly quickly
too. Only a day in Bear Paw, and already somebody was out
to kill Ryerson. It could only be one of the men he'd been
asking about, or somebody who was working with them.
Longarm felt like the solution to the whole mystery was
tantalizingly close, somewhere in the shadows around him.

He stopped and listened intently, knowing that his ears
were just as valuable as his eyes in a situation such as this,
maybe even more so. Off to the south, on the other side of
the tracks, a lot of loud voices cluttered the night. It was
quieter over here where he was.

That was why he was able to hear the stealthy scuff of
leather on ground behind him. He dove forward, twisting
as he went down, and flame lanced through the darkness. A
bullet cut through the space where he had been a heartbeat
earlier. Longarm fired, aiming low, hoping he could knock
the gunman's legs out from under him. Instead he heard
the swift patter of steps as the gunman ran again.

Biting back a curse, Longarm surged up from the
ground. He was about to give chase when something
slammed into him from the side. He went down again, feeling the weight of a man on top of him. Before he could try

132

to throw that weight off, a gun barrel jabbed into his side, and a familiar voice ordered, "Surrender, or I'll be forced to shoot!"

"Damn it, Ryerson, it's me!" Longarm grated.

The gun went away, and Ryerson pushed himself to his feet. "Good Lord!" the Mountie exclaimed. "Are you all right?"

"Yeah, just got the wind knocked out of me." Longarm grasped the hand that Ryerson held down toward him, and he got up with the constable's help. "That son of a bitch is long gone by now."

"Yes, I'm afraid you're right. We've missed our opportunity."

"This one anyway," said Longarm. "Were you hit when he first opened fire on you?"

Ryerson touched his left arm. "Just grazed. I'll be fine."

Longarm grunted. "If they want you dead bad enough to bushwhack you, chances are they'll try again."

"Yes, there is that bit of good news," Ryerson said, and Longarm couldn't tell if the constable was being sarcastic or not. Somehow, he didn't think so.

"I'm getting out of here," Longarm said quickly. "Folks don't need to see me trying to give you a hand."

"That's right. We'll rendezvous tomorrow, as planned."

With a curt nod that he didn't know if Ryerson saw or not, Longarm holstered his gun and faded off into the shadows. He circled wide, heading back toward the south side of the tracks and the Saskatchewan Palace.

By the time he pushed back the canvas flap and walked into the big tent, the place was buzzing. He heard snatches of conversation from the, excited railroaders: "—bushwhacked—" "—tried to kill that Mountie—" "—ambushed him right in the street—"

Longarm didn't hear any comments about *his* part in the shooting scrape, though, and he was glad of that. Obviously, by the time anybody had taken a look to see what all the gunfire was about, he had been on his way after the bushwhacker and no one had noticed him.

When Longarm came up to the bar, Rufus said, "Have you heard? Somebody took some shots at that Mountie who was in here a while ago." Rufus's bushy eyebrows suddenly arched as a thought occurred to him. "Say! You left here with that fella. You didn't have anything to do with . . . ?"

"Hell, no," Longarm said. "He just bullied me a little, asked me a few questions, and then told me to go on my way. I heard some shooting a few minutes later, but I didn't have any idea what it was about until I got back here."

"Is that right?" Rufus looked skeptical. "Took you a while to get here, didn't it?"

Rufus wasn't dumb. And the questions he was asking would likely occur to other people too. Longarm took out a cheroot, lit it, and then said around the smoke, "I had to see a man about a horse."

"Right."

Let Rufus think whatever he wanted to. Let other folks be suspicious of him too. If they believed he had tried to ventilate Constable Ryerson, they sure wouldn't wonder if he was really working with the Mounted Policeman. Suspicion, in this case, was a good thing.

Maybe if the men who wanted Ryerson dead heard talk about how the new bouncer at the Saskatchewan Palace had a grudge against the Mountie, they might decide to approach him, just to feel him out and see if he would be interested in settling a personal score with Ryerson and earning some money at the same time. Wouldn't that be an interesting turn of events, Longarm thought.

If he was lucky, the men he was after might come to him—and ask him to kill the Mountie who was snooping around Bear Paw.

Chapter 16

The rest of the night passed relatively quietly. Longarm was called on a couple of times to quiet down some railroad workers who drank too much and got a mite obstreperous, but those were the only duties he had to fulfill in his job as a troubleshooter for the Saskatchewan Palace. Around two in the morning, Queenie wrapped her shawl around her shoulders and left for her tent, turning the place over to Longarm and Rufus. Not surprisingly, she didn't invite Longarm to accompany her, since her father still lay in the tent, hovering between life and death.

Late in the night, when the Palace finally closed, Longarm went back to Claude Renoir's tent and found the French-Canadian already up cooking breakfast. Longarm shoved a couple of benches together and pitched his bedroll on them as Claude had suggested, and he got about three hours of sleep before dawn broke and hungry customers began flocking into the tent.

"I am sorry, *m'sieu*," Claude said as a groggy Longarm helped himself to a cup of coffee from the pot. "When I offered to let you stay here, I did not think about the differences in the hours we keep."

"I'm obliged anyway, Claude," Longarm said. He took a sip of the strong, bracing coffee and felt a little better. "It sure as hell ain't your fault."

"You want some breakfast?"

"I sure do." Longarm knew a hearty meal would make him feel stronger despite the lack of sleep.

While he was eating, a big, blond, hatless man in an expensive suit came into the tent. He looked vaguely familiar to Longarm. The man stood just inside the entrance for a moment, looking around, and then his gaze fell on Longarm. He surprised the big lawman by starting toward him. As the man strode along the table, Longarm remembered where he had seen him before. He was one of the men who had been in the train car with Clarence Rossley when Longarm went there to fetch the doctor.

"Mr. Parker?" the man asked as he came up to Longarm.

"That's right," Longarm said with a nod.

"Jasper Chamberlain," the man introduced himself. He shook hands with Longarm. "I've been looking for you. Mr. Rossley would like to speak with you."

"Is that so?" Longarm replied coolly. "What makes you think I want to palaver with Mr. High-and-Mighty Rossley?"

Chamberlain grinned. "Clarence *can* be a little full of himself at times, I'll admit. But he has a lot of responsibility weighing on him. I'm his personal secretary, and you would certainly make my job a lot easier if you came along with me and spoke to him."

Longarm eyed the tall, muscular man. "Personal secretary, eh? You look more like you ought to be swinging a maul and driving spikes."

"I used to do that very thing a long time ago," Chamberlain said. "I educated myself, though, and now I work at less strenuous tasks."

Longarm had to admit to himself that he was curious. He didn't know why the construction superintendent would want to see him. There was only one way to find out, though.

"Sure, I'll go with you," he said. "Just let me finish my breakfast."

"No hurry. Well, not too much of one anyway."

Longarm ate the last few bites on his plate and drank the last of his coffee. He put the plate and cup in the wash barrel and said to Renoir, "See you later, Claude." Then he followed Chamberlain out of the tent.

Work was already under way on the railroad. The construction train had moved a mile or so down the freshly laid tracks. Chamberlain motioned to a handcar and said, "That's what brought me here. Have you ever ridden on one before?"

"Pumped many a mile on one just like this down in the States," Longarm replied as both men climbed onto the handcar.

"So you've been a railroader?"

"I've been a lot of things," Longarm said vaguely.

Chamberlain didn't press the point. He and Longarm grasped the handles at each end of the seesawlike beam in the middle of the handcar and began pumping it up and down, alternating their effort. The handcar started to roll toward the construction train.

Once they had some speed built up, the going was a lot easier and required less effort. It took them about ten minutes to reach the construction train. They stopped pumping soon enough so that the handcar eased to a halt only a few feet from the locomotive's cowcatcher. The big engine with its diamond stack was pointed back east along the track toward the tent settlement. When it came time to move the train of boxcars and flatcars farther west along the tracks, the locomotive would go into reverse and push the train that direction.

Longarm and Chamberlain hopped down from the handcar and walked past the engine and the coal tender to the passenger cars that served as construction headquarters. Longarm looked along the train—the big boxcars that served as rolling barracks for the workers, a couple of windowless boxcars that were no doubt used for storage of some sort, and the numerous open flatcars filled with rails and ties and other supplies. It took a lot of men and material to build a railroad. In many ways, it was a monumental undertaking. The steel rails were greased with plenty of blood and sweat and not a few tears. But in the end, when the line spanned the entire continent from east to west, all the trouble would be worth it, Longarm supposed. Down in the States, the completion of the transcontinental railroad had really opened up the West as nothing before it had, not even the Gold Rush.

Longarm followed Chamberlain up the steps and into the first passenger car. Rossley was there, along with a natty little man who also wore an expensive suit like Chamberlain and stood by the table, leaning on a cane. "Mr. Parker," Rossley greeted him with an outstretched hand. "Thank you for coming. I'm sorry I was a bit high-handed with you yesterday. I realize now you were just trying to help that Drummond fella after he'd been shot. How is he doing by the way?"

Longarm shook hands with the construction superintendent. "Last I heard, he was still alive, but just barely."

"Well, I hope he pulls through." Rossley sniffed. "To tell you the truth, I don't have much use for all the saloon-keepers and gamblers and painted women who have followed us across the plains, but I don't wish them any personal harm, you understand."

"Sure," said Longarm. He still wondered what the hell Rossley wanted with him.

Rossley turned and indicated the small man who stood at the table behind him. "Simon McDermott, our auditor."

McDermott nodded to Longarm and said pleasantly, "Howdy."

Still puzzled, Longarm returned the nod. As far as Rossley and the others knew, he was just a saloon tough, hired to keep the peace in the Saskatchewan Palace. Why were they being so damned polite to him?

"To tell you the truth," Rossley went on, "I'll be very glad when the Mounted Police close down all those sordid establishments and force them to move out at least five miles from the rail line."

Longarm couldn't help but frown. How in blazes did Rossley know about that? Then the answer hit him. Constable Ryerson had told him, of course. Ryerson had spent quite a bit of time with the construction superintendent after arriving in Bear Paw, and naturally he had put his cards on the table with the man.

But just how much had Ryerson told him?

"I don't reckon I know what you're talking about," Longarm said cautiously. "What's this about five miles?"

Rossley smiled and said, "Come now, Marshal. That *is* the proper way to address you, isn't it? Constable Ryerson told us that you're a United States marshal."

Well, that was plain enough, thought Longarm. Ryerson had spilled everything. But maybe that was a good thing. It might not hurt to have the railroad bosses on their side, although if it had been up to Longarm, he probably would have kept his real identity quiet for a while longer.

"Deputy marshal actually," Longarm said. "Sounds like you and the Mountie had a good talk."

"Yes, he explained that the two of you are looking for some women who were kidnapped down below the border." Rossley motioned toward the table where the maps were spread out. "Sit down, Marshal. Would you like a drink?"

"It's a mite early in the day for that, ain't it?"

Rossley shrugged. "I just so happen to have a bottle of fine Maryland rye, and I've been looking for an excuse to crack it open."

139

Longarm rubbed his jaw and then said, "Well, I reckon it's not *too* early."

Rossley motioned to Chamberlain. The burly secretary fetched a bottle from a cabinet, along with four glasses. Rossley poured drinks for everyone, and then as the four men settled around the table, he said to Longarm, "Tell us what you've found out, Marshal."

Between sips of the Maryland rye, which was mighty smooth and good, Longarm filled them in on the investigation that had taken him from Fort Shaw, in Montana Territory, to the spanking-new settlement of Bear Paw in Saskatchewan. Rossley, Chamberlain, and McDermott all shook their heads grimly as Longarm detailed the kidnappings.

"That's terrible," Rossley said. "And you think those women were brought up here and forced to work as prostitutes?"

"That's the only explanation that makes any sense," Longarm said. "The fact that somebody took a shot at Ryerson last night tells me we're on the right trail too."

Rossley leaned forward. "I believe you're correct about that, Marshal. And I hope we can help you."

"How's that?"

"After Constable Ryerson talked to me, I asked around among the men." Rossley grimaced a little. "Rather, I should say I had the boss of one of my section gangs ask around. The men probably wouldn't tell me about some whorehouse they've been patronizing."

Rossley was likely right about that, thought Longarm. Workers were never too forthcoming with the big bosses about anything . . . but they might open up to somebody who swung a maul and toted rails right along with them.

"Got a spy or two among the men, eh?" Longarm asked with a grin.

Rossley looked pained again. "A necessary evil, Marshal. At any rate, what I found out is that there's a new place where some of the men have been going. All of the women there are young. Some of them are very young. Distastefully young."

Longarm felt his interest quicken. That sounded like what he was looking for, all right. "Is this place in Bear Paw?"

Rossley shook his head and said, "No, that's why you haven't been able to find it. The women are being kept in a cabin a couple of miles south of here. But the men are willing to borrow a horse or even walk that far if they have to, in order to have a chance at these fresh young women."

"Son of a bitch," Longarm grated. He looked from Rossley to Chamberlain to McDermott. After all this time, he had just been handed the solution to the case that had brought him to Canada.

"Indeed," Rossley said. "I imagine the men you're looking for can be found at that cabin as well. Are you and Constable Ryerson going to ride down there and arrest them and free those women?"

"I'll have to talk to Ryerson first, but I imagine that's just what we'll do, probably tonight."

Rossley nodded toward Chamberlain. "Take Jasper with you. He's a good man in a fight."

Chamberlain grinned and lifted a big fist, looking eager to get in on the finish of this business.

"I don't know about that," Longarm said. "He ain't a sworn peace officer, like the constable and me."

"Then take him along as a representative of the Canadian Pacific Railroad," Rossley suggested. "Surely the railroad has a stake in this affair too. If it weren't for our construction workers, those women never would have been kidnapped."

"And you're thinking that if the story gets out, it'll be a black eye for the railroad. Might not seem as bad, though, if somebody from the CP helped round up the bastards responsible."

Rossley shrugged. "My job is not only to get this railroad built, but also to make sure no one has a reason to regret riding it."

Longarm thought it over for a moment and then nodded. "All right, Chamberlain can come along. I'll send word later where and when to meet us, after I've talked to Ryerson."

"Excellent," Rossley said. "Thank you, Marshal."

"Reckon you're the one who should be getting thanked," Longarm said. "Without your help, Ryerson and me would still be stumbling around in the dark."

Rossley stood. "I'm glad I was able to give you a hand. This is just a start, though. When Inspector Steele and his Mounties come in and clean up that Hell on Wheels that's been following us, you'll see the work go faster and better than ever."

"I don't reckon I'll see it," Longarm said.

Rossley frowned. "Why not?"

"Because by then I figure I'll be back down in the States, chasing some other bunch of badmen my boss has sent me after." Longarm shook his head. "Seems like no matter how many owlhoots a fella catches, there's always another bunch just waiting to raise hell and shove a chunk under the corner."

Chapter 17

After leaving the railroad car, Longarm climbed back on the handcar with one of the workers Rossley picked out to go with him, and they pumped it back along the tracks to Bear Paw. Longarm climbed off, waved his thanks to the railroader, and headed for the Saskatchewan Palace. It was late enough in the morning by now so that a few people would probably be at the saloon. He hoped to find Queenie or Rufus and find out if Clive Drummond had made it through the night. He was still curious about what Drummond had been about to tell him just before the shooting started. He might never know, though, if Drummond succumbed to his injury.

At the same time, Longarm was turning over in his mind everything he had learned this morning. The men he was after had put together a neat scheme, sure enough, and no doubt it would have made them rich if it had been successful. They were in for a surprise, though, and Longarm was going to enjoy springing it on them.

Rufus was leaning sleepily on the bar when Longarm came into the tent. He looked up and yawned. "Mornin', Custis," he said. "You're out and about early."

143

"Not that early," Longarm said. "You heard anything about how Mr. Drummond is doing?"

"Queenie was just here a few minutes ago. Drummond's still alive. Accordin' to Queenie, the doc says that if he makes it through another day or two, then he's got a fightin' chance."

Longarm nodded. By then, even if Drummond lived, the case would be wrapped up, he hoped. But maybe he could still satisfy his curiosity and find out what Drummond knew about it.

He chatted with Rufus for a while longer and then walked along the street to the corral. The bandy-legged little proprietor grinned at him and asked, "Gonna exercise your horse again?"

"That's right. You never know when you're going to need to ride somewhere in a hurry."

"That's sure enough true," the man agreed. "I'll fetch your saddle."

A few minutes later, Longarm rode out of Bear Paw, heading north. Having followed this trail only the day before, he had no difficulty reaching the site of Ryerson's camp by midday. Not surprisingly, he found the constable waiting for him. Ryerson's left arm was stiff from the bullet crease he had received the previous night, but the wound didn't appear to be bothering him too much.

"Hello, Marshal," Ryerson greeted Longarm as the big lawman swung down from the saddle. "Have you discovered anything since we last spoke?"

"Well, you could say that," Longarm drawled. "I know where those women are being held, and I know who's responsible for kidnapping them and bringing them up here."

Ryerson's eyes widened. Even his normally unflappable exterior was shaken by Longarm's matter-of-fact declaration. "For God's sake, man, tell me!" the Mountie exclaimed.

Longarm did so, laying out everything for Ryerson. The

constable listened intently, at first skeptical but then finally nodding in agreement.

"You're right, of course. It's all quite simple when you stop and think about it. Shocking, but simple."

"We'll put a stop to it tonight," said Longarm. "Meet me at Rossley's railroad car around dusk. We'll pick up Chamberlain there and head south."

"Agreed." A faint smile appeared on Ryerson's face. "Try not to get in any trouble between now and then, Marshal. I would hate it if you came this far and then missed the showdown."

"Take it from me," Longarm said with a grin, "I wouldn't be too fond of it myself."

Queenie came into the Saskatchewan Palace that afternoon while Longarm was sitting at one of the tables laying out a hand of solitaire in front of him. She motioned for Rufus to bring over a bottle, then went to the table and joined Longarm. He stood up and held her chair for her.

"You're a gentleman, Custis," she said. "I could tell that about you the first time I saw you . . . along with a few other things."

Longarm let that comment pass and asked, "How's your father?"

"As well as can be expected," Queenie said. "He hasn't regained consciousness, but Dr. Davis isn't surprised at that. The doctor has been pretty good about coming by to check on him."

"Well, we'll keep him in our thoughts and hope El Señor Dios watches over him."

"That's an odd expression."

"What?"

"El Señor Dios."

Longarm shrugged. "Down in the border country in Texas, New Mexico, and Arizona, you hear it a lot. Plenty of Spanish-speaking folks down there. Up here you got folks like Claude Renoir, who I reckon speaks French. It keeps things spiced up, having folks around from all over."

"I suppose so. You've been all over yourself, haven't you, Custis?"

"What makes you say that?"

"You just have that look about you," Queenie said with a smile. "The look of a man who's been places and done things."

Longarm inclined his head. "I reckon that's true enough."

Rufus brought over a bottle and glasses. Queenie said that she would pour the drinks, and she did so, clinking her glass against Longarm's before she drank.

"To the future of Bear Paw," she said. "We have a load of lumber coming in next week. We'll start building a permanent structure. When it's finished we'll have the best saloon west of Winnipeg."

"I hope that works out for you," said Longarm.

Queenie tossed off her drink and looked squarely at him. "Have you thought any more about what we talked about yesterday?"

Longarm lowered his voice and asked, "You mean Frederick?"

"That's right."

"If your father lives, you don't have to worry about that, do you?"

"Clive's not out of the woods yet," Queenie said. "He may not recover."

"I've always found it best not to borrow trouble," said Longarm. "Wait and see what happens. Maybe you won't have to do anything."

"You're just stalling so you won't have to make up your mind," she accused.

She was wrong about that, thought Longarm. His mind was already made up, always had been. He wasn't going to kill Frederick Drummond for her. Even if he hadn't been a lawman, he wasn't a hired killer.

"Just wait and see," he told her again.

Queenie sighed in frustration. "You're not the only man in Bear Paw, you know."

"That's right. There's a Mountie in town too. So it'd be mighty damned foolish to be going around talking about killing folks, don't you reckon?"

Queenie picked up the bottle and splashed more whiskey into the glass. "I suppose you're right," she said grudgingly. "But I'm not going to let my uncle steal this place from me. No matter what happens, I won't allow that."

"I hope it never comes to that," Longarm said, and meant it.

Queenie left a short time later to go back to her tent and check on Drummond. Longarm drifted over to the bar and said to Rufus, "You'd better keep an eye on that little lady."

"Why's that?"

"She's mortally afraid that her uncle is going to wind up taking over this place if her pa dies. She's liable to do something foolish if that happens."

Rufus just stared at him for a moment before saying, "What in blazes are you talking about, Custis?"

Longarm realized then that he had revealed a secret. Well, it was too late to call back now, he reasoned, so he said quietly, "Clive Drummond is Queenie's father."

Rufus's eyes widened in surprise. "Good Lord!" he muttered. "I been workin' for Drummond for three years and never knew that. I thought Queenie and him were . . . well, you know. . . ."

Longarm nodded. "I thought the same thing at first. But she's his daughter, sure enough."

Rufus frowned in thought and tugged on his beard. "That makes things a mite different. I've always thought

Queenie was awful pretty and nice, but I never . . . well, I figured I never had a chance, eh?"

"Stranger things been known to happen, old son," Longarm said sagely.

Once he left Canada behind and returned to the States, his mind would rest a mite easier knowing that Rufus was looking out for Queenie. He wasn't sure if Rufus was strong enough to stand up to Queenie's feisty nature, but the big bartender seemed to be the most likely candidate around here.

"I'll have to think on this," Rufus said.

"You do that," Longarm advised him. With that, he left the Saskatchewan Palace, walked over to Claude's, and ate a late lunch. The French-Canadian asked him about Clive Drummond, and Longarm passed along the information he knew.

Then he said, "I hear that the Saskatchewan Palace is going to have a permanent building as soon as the lumber gets here and they can put it up. You ever think about putting down roots here in Bear Paw, Claude?"

"*Oui*. I think this will be a good town once the railhead moves on. I would like to stay."

"Seems to me like the little fella over at the corral would make a good citizen of a real town too."

Claude bobbed his head in agreement. "Jeremy Stubbs is his name. I will talk to him and see what his plans are."

"Round up some of the other folks who have businesses here and see what they think," Longarm advised. "You'll come closer to the settlement making a go of it if you have some plans."

Enthusiastically, Claude slapped a big palm down on the table. "*Mais oui!* Perhaps you would remain here too, M'sieu Parker. If we are to be a real town, we will need an officer of the law."

That was hitting pretty close to the mark, thought Longarm, but he didn't congratulate Claude on his perception.

Instead he just grinned and shook his head. "I'll have to be moving on long before that time comes around, but you'll find the man you need. Let the gamblers and the crooks go with the railroad. If you get enough solid, decent folks together, this will be a fine little town."

"*Certainment.* Thank you for your ideas, M'sieu Parker."

"Always glad to help," Longarm said with a smile.

He dawdled there for a couple of hours, talking to Claude. Then, as the late afternoon light began to fade, Longarm took his leave and strolled back to the corral.

"Ridin' out again?" Jeremy Stubbs asked in surprise.

"That's right," Longarm said. "Got to take care of a little business."

He didn't add that his business was with a bunch of kidnappers and would-be killers.

When he had his horse saddled, he mounted up and rode along the railroad tracks toward the construction train. He hadn't seen Constable Ryerson since their meeting in the middle of the day, but when he reached the train, he found the Mountie waiting for him.

Clarence Rossley, Jasper Chamberlain, and Simon McDermott were there as well, McDermott leaning on his cane. Chamberlain still wore his expensive suit, but he had buckled on a six-gun and was mounted on a big bay gelding.

"Would you like some more men to go with you, Marshal?" Rossley offered. "I could get some of the workers, and perhaps Constable Ryerson could swear them in as temporary constables, or something like that."

"I don't reckon that's necessary," Longarm said.

"I concur," Ryerson added. "Marshal Long and I should be able to handle this matter."

Chamberlain said, "I'll be along to lend a hand if you need me, gentlemen."

Longarm nodded. "That's right. Are we all ready to ride?"

Chamberlain and Ryerson both nodded.

"Lead the way then, Mr. Chamberlain," Longarm said to the man. "You know where we're going better than me and the constable do."

"Very well." Chamberlain swung his horse's head around and urged the animal into a trot. He rode south away from the railroad right-of-way, with Longarm and Ryerson riding beside him.

"You know how many men will be at this cabin where the women are being held?" Longarm asked when they had gone a half mile or so.

"According to Clarence's informant, there are usually just two men at the place."

"Probably the two who kidnapped the poor ladies in the first place," Ryerson put in.

"I suppose so. I wouldn't know about that."

The sun had set, but an orange glow still filled the western sky above some distant hills. Chamberlain pointed out those rounded heights and commented, "Those are the Cypress Hills. They shouldn't be too difficult to cross when the railroad comes to them. Not like the Rockies will be."

"I reckon the railroad will make it just fine," Longarm said. "Once an enterprise like that gets to rolling, it's hard to stop."

"I hope you're correct, Marshal. Canada needs this rail line."

They rode on and came to a narrow, fast-flowing stream. "Swiftcurrent Creek," Chamberlain said. "I know the names of these geographical features because I've studied the maps that Clarence has. Despite its isolation, this area has been well surveyed."

The three men followed the creek as night fell. Longarm figured they had gone three, maybe four miles from the railroad when he abruptly reined in and said, "I reckon that's far enough."

Ryerson and Chamberlain brought their mounts to a halt as well. Chamberlain looked over at Longarm in confusion. "What do you mean far enough, Marshal? We haven't reached the cabin yet. It should be another mile or so farther on."

Quickly, before Chamberlain knew what was going on, Longarm drew his gun and covered the burly railroad man. "The only thing a mile or so farther on is the ambush you've laid for us," he said. "And the constable and me don't plan on riding right into it like you and your pards planned, Chamberlain."

Chamberlain gaped at him.

"By the way, Mr. Chamberlain," Ryerson said as he moved his horse up on the man's other side with his gun drawn as well, "in the name of the Crown, you're under arrest."

Chapter 18

Chamberlain's mouth snapped shut. Even in the dim light, Longarm could see the anger and hatred on the man's broad face as he looked back and forth between the lawmen.

"How long have you known?" he asked in a grating voice.

"Just since earlier today," replied Longarm. "Why don't you reach across with your left hand and take out that hogleg, Chamberlain? Nice and easylike, and when you've got it, hand it over butt-first."

Chamberlain hesitated, but covered as he was by two guns, he had little choice but to follow Longarm's orders. As he reached across his body with his left hand, he said, "Who told you? Was it Simon? That little bastard—"

"It wasn't McDermott," Longarm said. "Or I guess you could say in a way it was both of you."

"Both of us!" Chamberlain exclaimed. Using his left hand, he drew the pistol on his hip from its holster.

"That's right. When I was sitting there in Rossley's railroad car looking at the two of you, I realized that I've been looking for a big fella and a little fella, and there you two were, right in front of me. Sure, you'd shaved your beard off and you were dressed in that fancy suit instead of an old

153

buffalo coat. And you weren't soft in the head like the big hombre who'd been described to me, but a smart man can always pretend to be dumb. McDermott shaved his goatee too, and put away his derby hat and went back to his original job, before he turned kidnapper."

Chamberlain extended the pistol toward Longarm butt-first. "You don't have a damn bit of proof for any of this," he accused.

"Once we go back to the railroad and unlock those closed-up boxcars where you've got the women hidden, I reckon their testimony will be all the proof we need." Longarm reached for the gun Chamberlain held out toward him.

With a flick of his wrist, Chamberlain sent the pistol spinning straight at Longarm's face. At the same time, he jabbed his heels into his horse's flanks, jerked on the reins, and sent the animal lunging against Ryerson's horse.

It was a desperate move, but Chamberlain was a desperate man. Ryerson fired and Chamberlain grunted as the bullet struck him. Chamberlain was able to stay in the saddle, though, and he leaned over his mount's neck as the horse plunged away in a wild gallop.

Longarm had instinctively ducked the thrown gun, but then he'd had to hold off on his trigger finger for fear of missing Chamberlain and hitting Ryerson. Now he jammed the Colt back in its holster and sent his horse racing after Chamberlain. Ryerson's horse was down, having been knocked off its hooves by the collision with Chamberlain's horse.

Chamberlain was still heading south, and Longarm knew what that meant: He was riding toward the bushwhackers that he and his partners had sent down here to kill Longarm and Ryerson. Longarm knew that if he and the constable hadn't acted when they did, Chamberlain would have found some reason to stop and send the two of them on alone to their deaths. Probably would have claimed that his horse had gone lame or something like that. But Longarm and Ryerson had made their move first, spoiling the plan.

Longarm didn't want Chamberlain to get away. The man might circle back to Bear Paw and try to warn Rossley and McDermott. Longarm never doubted for an instant that Rossley was in on the scheme. The whole thing might have even been his idea. Chamberlain and McDermott couldn't have pulled it off without the cooperation of the construction superintendent. They had a few of the railroaders working for them as well, because they would have needed help here and there.

McDermott had been the one who'd tried to kill Ryerson the night before, Longarm suspected. The accountant wasn't using a cane because he had a naturally bum leg; he used a cane because he'd been clipped by Longarm's bullet during the shoot-out near the railroad tracks. That theory had fallen into place once Longarm realized that Chamberlain and McDermott fit the descriptions of the men he'd been looking for. So had the presence of those closed-up boxcars. They had to be where the stolen women were imprisoned. Rossley and his partners could have cut ventilation holes in the floor so that the women could breathe, but it must have been a hellish existence for them anyway, shut up like that in darkness, probably gagged and tied, with no hope of escape. Just the thought of it made Longarm urge his horse on to greater speed.

He could see Chamberlain up ahead and hear the pounding of hoofbeats from the galloping horse. He wasn't the only one who could see and hear those things, Longarm realized a moment later as muzzle flashes suddenly split the darkness.

"No!" Chamberlain screamed as the bullets began to fly. "Don't shoot! Don't—"

His cries were cut off abruptly as more shots blasted. The men who were posted out here to ambush Longarm and Ryerson had their orders—they were to open fire on the first men who rode up. In his panic to get away, Chamberlain had forgotten about that . . . and now he had paid the price. He tumbled off his horse and landed on the ground with a limp, soggy thud.

Longarm reined in sharply and drew his Winchester from the saddle sheath. The bushwhackers began to fire at him too. He didn't know if they had figured out their mistake, or if they were just trying to kill the second man they'd been paid to ambush. He threw lead right back at them, aiming at the muzzle flashes.

He wasn't the only one putting up a fight. Rapid shots came from his left, but they weren't directed at him. Constable John Ryerson had gotten his horse back on its feet and caught up to Longarm. He joined the battle now, spraying bullets through the darkness from his own Winchester. The bushwhack lead stopped flying. As Longarm lowered his rifle, he heard the swift rataplan of retreating hoofbeats. At least one of the ambushers was taking off for the tall and uncut.

"Are you wounded, Marshal?" Ryerson asked.

"Nope. The bullets sounded like a swarm of bees around me for a minute, but none of 'em stung."

"Thank God for that. Where's Chamberlain?"

"He fell off his horse, looked like he was hit pretty bad. Reckon he forgot what he was doing and rode right into his own ambush."

"Well, I'm not going to waste any sympathy on him," Ryerson said crisply. "We had better check and be sure what happened to him, though."

They rode forward slowly, holding their rifles at the ready. The sound of a faint groan came to Longarm's ears, but it didn't originate with the dark lump on the ground that was Chamberlain's body. While Ryerson checked on Chamberlain, Longarm rode into the clump of low-lying brush where the bushwhackers had been hidden. The moaning continued.

"I think you're trying to trick me, old son," Longarm said in a loud, clear voice. "So I'm just gonna aim at the sound of those moans and empty this Winchester o' mine."

"N-no!" came a strangled, frantic reply. "D-don't shoot, mister! It ain't . . . a trick! I'm hit . . . bad . . ."

"What about the others?" asked Longarm, his voice every bit as hard-bitten as he felt right now. He didn't like being ambushed.

"Tully's d-dead. . . . Baird up an' . . . ran."

"There were just three of you?"

"Th-that's right. Oh, Lord, you gotta help me, mister! My gut's on fire!"

If the bushwhacking bastard was gut-shot, there wasn't much Longarm could do for him. The big lawman swung down from the saddle anyway and cautiously explored the brush until he found the sprawled body of the wounded man. The ambusher lay on his back with his hands pressed to his belly. There was enough light from the stars and the rising moon to reveal the huge black stain under his fingers. The son of a bitch didn't have long, thought Longarm.

"You and your pards work for the railroad?" asked Longarm as he stood over the dying man, keeping the Winchester trained on him.

"Y-yeah."

"Rossley sent you out here to kill me and that Mountie?"

"He . . . he said we had to . . . get rid of you . . . said it would be better to kill both of you . . . at the same time. . . . He was mad as hell . . .'cause Mr. McDermott passed up the chance last night . . . and just tried for that damned M-Mountie. . . ."

A crackling in the brush made Longarm turn his head, but it was just Ryerson coming up to him. "Chamberlain's dead," the constable reported. "So is another man a few yards over there." He swept his free hand toward the left.

"That'd be an hombre called Tully," Longarm said. "I don't know this fella's name, but him and his friends work

157

for the railroad when they ain't trying to ambush poor, hardworking lawmen."

"I . . . I'm sorry," the gut-shot man gasped. "For God's sake . . . can't you . . . do something for me?"

"What's your name?" asked Ryerson.

"D-Danielson."

"Well, I'm sorry, Mr. Danielson, but a belly wound such as the one you have almost invariably proves fatal. Even if there was a physician here right now, it's highly doubtful that you would live. We'll try to find your horse and take you back to Bear Paw, but I'm almost certain that you'll expire before we reach the settlement."

The wounded man rolled his head toward Longarm and pleaded, "Can't you just . . . shoot me in the head?"

"Wouldn't be proper for a lawman to do that," Longarm replied. "For what it's worth, though, I would if I could."

"You . . . son of a bitch. . . ."

Danielson cursed them both for about thirty seconds, then stopped abruptly, arched his back, said, "Mama!" and died.

"Well, that was a mite quicker than I thought it would be," Longarm said. "Son of a bitch was lucky."

Longarm and Ryerson were able to round up the horses belonging to the three dead men and load the corpses onto them. Once the bodies were tied in place, head-down over the saddle, the grim procession started toward Bear Paw.

"Do you think the man who got away will go back and warn Rossley and McDermott?" Ryerson asked.

"I think he sure might," replied Longarm, "so we may be riding smack-dab into another ambush."

"Perhaps we should split up. I'll take the bodies back into town. You ride ahead, circle around, and approach Bear Paw from the north. That way if they try to kill me, you can take them by surprise."

Longarm grunted. "You sure like to have a target plas-

158

tered on your chest, don't you, Ryerson? Must come from wearing that red coat all the time."

"We can do it the other way around, if you'd like," Ryerson said.

"I think we might ought to, this time."

"As you wish, Marshal." Ryerson handed over the reins of the horse he was leading. Longarm now had the reins of all three mounts carrying the bodies of Chamberlain and the dead bushwhackers. Ryerson lifted a hand to the brim of his hat. "Take your time getting back to Bear Paw, and that will give me a chance to get into position."

"Good enough," Longarm agreed. "I'll head straight for Rossley's railroad car."

"I'll be close by when you get there," Ryerson promised. With that, the constable rode off into the night.

Longarm moved along at a steady pace, leading the three horses, not hurrying, but not dawdling either. Ryerson had a good horse, and Longarm knew it wouldn't take the Mountie too long to circle around the settlement and slip up to the railroad from the north.

A short time later the lights of Bear Paw came into view. As Longarm rode closer, he angled toward the construction train and saw that lights burned in the windows of the passenger cars as well. A faint rumbling drifted over the prairie, and when Longarm heard it he recognized it as the sound of the locomotive. A frown creased his forehead. The engine had steam up. That was odd. There was no reason for the locomotive to be ready to roll at this time of night, unless—

"Damn it!" Longarm burst out as he dropped the reins of the horses carrying the dead bodies and jabbed his own mount in the flanks with his boot heels. The horse leaped forward.

The locomotive wouldn't have steam up unless Rossley had ordered it. And the only reason Rossley would order such a thing was if he intended to move the train tonight.

The third bushwhacker had made it back to Bear Paw, all right, and had warned the crooked construction superintendent. Now Rossley was going to make a run for it the best way he knew how—by train.

Longarm galloped hard, wondering where Ryerson was. Had the Mountie reached the railhead and figured out that Rossley was going to bolt? Longarm had no way of knowing. The only thing certain was that he had to stop that train before it pulled out.

But he was going to be too late for that, he realized grimly. As he raced closer, he heard the hiss of steam and then the clatter of steel on steel as the drivers engaged. The massive locomotive, hulking in the darkness like some beast from the dim recesses of prehistory, lurched forward and began to roll slowly along the tracks. Longarm heard another racket as the second of the closed-up boxcars came loose from the barracks car behind it. Somebody had uncoupled them, so that the locomotive was pulling only the coal tender, the two passenger cars, and the two boxcars.

Rossley was taking the women with him, the son of a bitch!

Longarm turned his horse and leaned forward over the animal's neck, trying to get more speed. The train was going faster now, its wheels clicking over the rails as it rolled toward the tent town. Longarm steered his mount at an angle toward the rails, flashing past the abandoned barracks cars and the flatcars piled high with supplies. The second boxcar was about fifty yards ahead of him, but the train was still picking up speed.

The locomotive thundered between the scattered tents. Longarm rode alongside the rails, paying no attention to the shouts of the people in Bear Paw who witnessed this desperate race. The horse lunged forward gallantly, eating up huge chunks of ground with every stride. The valiant animal had cut the gap, but it might not be enough. Smoke from the stack plumed back along the train and stung

Longarm's nose and eyes as he rode through it. He felt cinders hitting his face. He leaned out from the saddle, stretching with his left hand for the nearest grab-iron on the back of the boxcar. It was still out of reach, and as Longarm's fingers fell short, he felt the horse finally begin to falter underneath him.

Well, hell, he thought. There was only one thing to do.

He kicked his feet free of the stirrups and left the saddle in a lunging dive, reaching out as far as he could.

Chapter 19

It wasn't quite as big a boneheaded play as it might have looked like. Longarm's first effort to reach the grab-iron had fallen only inches short. He had done things like this before and knew that he could do it again.

But still, during those interminable couple of seconds while he seemed to hang motionless in midair, stretching out his arms as far as possible, the image of him plowing face-first into the roadbed and busting the hell out of himself flashed through his mind.

Then his hands slapped against the grab-iron and closed around it with desperate strength. His hat flew off as he was jerked forward. His shoulder sockets groaned in protest as his weight tried to rip the bones apart.

Longarm hung on, willing his muscles to pull his legs up so that his booted feet wouldn't drag on the roadbed and perhaps catch on a cross-tie, maybe breaking his ankle or jolting his grip loose on the grab-iron. He lifted his head and looked up for the next iron. Tightening his left hand, he let go with his right and reached up.

Once he had hold of that one, he was able to pull himself high enough for his feet to get a grip on a lower iron. Then it was just a matter of climbing up them like a ladder.

A few moments later, Longarm pulled himself up and over the top, sprawling full-length on the roof of the boxcar.

Veteran brakemen probably got used to clambering around on the tops of trains, but Longarm had done it more than once in his life and didn't care for it. Even the steadiest train swayed back and forth a little, and it might take a sudden jolt that would throw a fella right off if he had been foolish enough to stand up and walk on his feet. That was why, after catching his breath, Longarm started toward the front of the train on hands and knees.

When he reached the other end of the boxcar, he came up in a crouch, spreading his feet wide and keeping one hand down on the roof to steady himself. There was no way to reach the other car without jumping the four-foot gap between them. It shouldn't be that hard a jump, he told himself, but a miss would send him toppling off the side, or worse, dropping between the boxcars to be cut to ribbons underneath them.

He had come this far. He was damned if he was going to quit now.

Longarm's muscles uncoiled smoothly and sent him flying through the air. He landed easily on the other boxcar and flattened out atop it, grabbing the roof. As he lay there, he wondered if the women being held prisoner in the car below him had heard the thump of his landing on the roof.

Somebody had sure heard it. That was confirmed a second later when a bullet punched through the roof about a foot to the right of his head. There was a gunman standing guard down there, and he wasn't taking any chances.

So much for being careful, Longarm thought as he surged to his feet and ran for the next car.

More slugs blasted through the roof of the boxcar, but he was able to stay ahead of them by running hard. When he reached the front end of the car, he didn't slow down. Like a big-ass bird, he sailed up and out, leaping for the roof of the next car in line, which was one of the tandem passenger cars.

He landed awkwardly and slid toward the edge. A lunging grab gave Longarm a handhold that allowed him to stop his slide. He pulled himself to the center of the car, then doodlebugged back to the awning over the rear platform. He swung his legs over and started down the ladder.

A gun roared almost in his face, half-deafening him. He heard the whine as the bullet ricocheted off metal. Dropping to the platform, he landed in a crouch that saved his life as Simon McDermott fired again from the rear door of the car. The slug screamed over Longarm's head, almost close enough to part his hair.

Instinct sent his hand flashing across his body to the butt of his Colt. He palmed out the revolver, tipped up the barrel, and fired. The bullet was traveling at an upward angle as it hit McDermott in the throat, bored on through his brain, and burst out the back of his head in a grisly shower of blood, bone, and gray matter. McDermott sat down hard in the open rear doorway of the railroad car and then fell lifelessly to the side.

Longarm powered up out of his crouch and leaped over McDermott's body into the car. The Colt tracked from side to side as the big lawman's keen eyes searched for any sign of another threat.

Instead he saw only the slender figure of Dr. Davis slumped in one of the seats. Blood had run down one side of the doctor's face from a gash in his forehead where he had been pistol-whipped. He was only half-conscious.

Longarm paused beside Davis and grasped his shoulder, shaking it lightly. "Doc! Doc, are you all right?"

Davis put a hand to his injured head and groaned. "What?" he asked fuzzily. He looked up, blinked several times, and finally focused on Longarm. "Parker!"

"The name's actually Custis Long, Doc," Longarm explained. "I'm a deputy marshal from down in the States. Who walloped you?"

"It was . . . ohhh . . . Rossley." Davis pulled a handkerchief from his pocket and wiped away some of the blood from his face as his strength began to come back to him. "He was like a madman. One of the workers came riding in . . . a man called Baird, I think . . . and spoke to Rossley. Then he ordered the engineer and the fireman to start getting steam up. . . . Did you say you're a marshal?"

"That's right." Longarm's voice was flat and hard as he went on. "I've been working with the Mounties. Rossley was behind a scheme to kidnap a bunch of women down in the States, bring 'em up here, and make whores out of 'em."

Davis stared at him uncomprehendingly. "Women? I don't understand. . . ."

"Take my word for it, Doc, Rossley's as crooked as a dog's hind leg and cold-blooded as a snake."

"I can believe it," muttered Davis, "after the way he pulled his gun and hit me when I demanded to know what was going on." He clutched at Longarm's sleeve. "You'll stop him?"

"Do my damnedest," Longarm vowed. "Are you all right now?"

Davis waved a hand. "Yes, I'll be fine. Go on, Marshal. Go ahead and arrest him. Just be careful. He's liable to shoot at you."

"Wouldn't be the first time," Longarm said as he turned toward the door at the front of the car. "By the way, Doc, Simon McDermott's back there dead. He was in on it too."

"McDermott! My God! I was surrounded by treachery and never even knew it!"

That was about the size of it, all right, thought Longarm as he started forward again. As a matter of fact, he had wondered briefly if the doctor might have been part of the scheme with Rossley, Chamberlain, and McDermott. The bloody wound on Davis's head had convinced Longarm that the sawbones was innocent.

He reached the door at the front end of the car, grasped the knob, and flung it open, lifting the Colt in his other hand in case Rossley was lurking on the other side. The platform was empty, though, and so was the rear platform on the next car. Longarm stepped across and tried that door. Locked. He braced himself with his left hand on the railing around the little platform, lifted his right leg, and drove his heel against the door. The kick slammed it open.

No shots came at him. Crouching, Longarm went through the door and looked along the car. It was empty. Where the hell was Rossley?

There was no other place for him to have gone except the engine. Longarm hurried to the front door of the car and kicked it open too. There was nothing between him and the locomotive now except the coal tender.

A narrow walkway ran along the side of the coal tender, but Longarm didn't use it. Instead he holstered his gun and climbed the ladder to the top of the car, which was open so that coal could be loaded into it easily. He began to clamber over the heaped-up mound of black chunks. He hoped the noises he made as the coal shifted under his feet would be drowned out by the rumble of the engine.

When he reached the top of the coal pile, he could see ahead of him into the cab of the locomotive. Rossley stood there with his back to Longarm. The crooked construction superintendent had a revolver in his hand, and he held it so that it menaced both the engineer and the fireman. Just as Longarm had suspected, Rossley had forced the train crew to cooperate with him. Longarm didn't know what Rossley intended to do with the captive women now that his scheme had been exposed. Use them as hostages probably, until he thought he had gotten away safely.

That wasn't going to happen. Longarm worked his way closer.

Then luck took a bad turn for him, as the engineer glanced back for some reason and spotted him crouching atop the mounded coal. The man's eyes widened in surprise, and that was enough to warn Rossley. Alertly, he swung around and brought up his gun.

Longarm dropped to a knee and reached for his Colt, but Rossley's gun was already out and lined up on him. A tongue of flame licked out from the muzzle as Rossley fired, and what felt like a giant hand punched Longarm on the right thigh. The impact knocked him back and onto his side. The shot that he fired instinctively in return whined off harmlessly into the sky.

Rossley came closer, firing with each step. Longarm's right leg was numb, but he kicked out with his left leg and rolled toward the side of the tender. Bullets spanked off the coal, searching for him but not quite finding him. Suddenly there was nothing underneath him, and he was dropping through the air.

He realized that he had rolled right off the coal tender. His feet hit the walkway, and he grabbed for a handhold to keep from toppling all the way to the ground. His right foot slipped and he almost fell again, but then he caught hold of a stanchion and hung on for dear life.

That life might not last too much longer. Rossley leaned out from the side of the cab and opened fire on him again. Longarm ducked as slugs sizzled around him and ricocheted screamingly from the metal sides of the coal car. He was like the proverbial sitting duck, stuck here, unable to go forward or backward, and unarmed now because he had dropped his Colt when he fell off the top of the coal mound.

Suddenly the train lurched heavily, almost throwing Longarm off. Its wheels screamed like imps of Hades against the steel rails as the locomotive slewed to a jolting halt. The engineer had taken a chance and thrown on the brakes, and that had flung Rossley off his feet and given Longarm a chance too.

His right leg was no longer numb. Now it hurt like blazes instead, but it worked and he knew as he scrambled along the walkway that Rossley's first shot had barely grazed him. When Longarm reached the front of the coal tender, he saw that Rossley was still down. The fireman swung his shovel at the crooked superintendent, but Rossley jerked out of the way and triggered a shot. The fireman lurched back, dropping his shovel and clutching a bloody upper arm.

Longarm flung himself at Rossley and grabbed the wrist of his gun hand, forcing it down and slamming it against the floor of the cab. Rossley cried out in pain as the gun slipped from his fingers and skittered across the cab. With his other hand he sledged a punch into the side of Longarm's head. The blow half-stunned the marshal. Rossley shoved him aside and crawled toward the pistol.

Longarm shook the cobwebs out of his head and dove after Rossley, tackling him from behind him. Both of them sprawled out and slid toward the edge of the cab. They toppled over and dropped toward the ground.

Longarm's left shoulder smashed painfully against the metal step as he fell. He bit back a curse as he rolled down the slight incline of the roadbed. Rossley had landed a few feet away and was also shaken up by the fall. Both men clambered to their feet at about the same time. His chest heaving, Rossley glowered at Longarm and yelled, "You bastard! You've ruined everything!"

"Ruined your scheme to kidnap those women and make whores out of them, you mean," Longarm said as he tried to work some feeling back into his left arm.

"We would have made a fortune! Once the Mounties clean out all the saloons and brothels, the women who worked for me would have been the only ones in a ten-mile-wide strip!"

"And you'd have kept them hidden in those boxcars and charged the men whatever you wanted," said Longarm. "You knew about the new orders the Mounted Police are about to put into effect. You knew you could clean up by running your own private whorehouse. All you had to do was come up with some whores, so you sent Chamberlain and McDermott down to Montana to steal some for you!"

"It would have worked too, damn you!"

"You might as well give it up, Rossley. I know about the scheme, and so does Constable Ryerson. Chamberlain and McDermott are both dead. You're the only one left."

Rossley hesitated. "I didn't kill anybody, and I didn't kidnap those women. I knew about it, but that's not the same as actually doing it. Chamberlain and McDermott forced me into helping them."

Longarm knew that wasn't true. He was more convinced than ever that Rossley had come up with the whole thing. But Longarm knew he couldn't prove that. Rossley had forced the engineer and fireman to move the train at gunpoint, and he had shot and wounded both Longarm and the fireman, but those were crimes that would get him a little jail time, not a hang rope. If he was smart enough to go ahead and surrender now, he might be a free man in a year or two. Of course, he would have lost his railroad job, but that would be better than a long prison term or the gallows.

And if nothing else, Clarence Rossley was a smart man. He lifted his hands and said, "I give up, Marshal. Take me into custody."

Longarm started toward him, filled with bitter frustration that Rossley was going to escape most of what was coming to him. But then Rossley's right arm snapped down and moonlight glinted on the stubby barrel of the derringer that slid from a gambler's hideout rig under his sleeve. The move didn't take Longarm completely by surprise. He had used his own derringer in a similar fashion more than once. He flung himself to the side as the derringer gave a wicked little bark and flame lanced from its barrel.

A heavier gun roared somewhere behind Longarm. He heard the thud of lead against flesh, and looked up to see Rossley stagger back a step. Rossley dropped the derringer and pressed his hand to his chest. He groaned a curse and then fell to his knees. Blood, black in the moonlight, welled between his fingers. After a moment he pitched forward onto his face and lay still.

Longarm pushed himself upright as he heard the crunch of hurrying footsteps on the gravel of the roadbed. He looked around to see the tall, erect figure of Constable John Ryerson coming toward him. Smoke still curled from the barrel of the pistol in Ryerson's hand.

"He gave me no choice," the Mountie said as he came up to Longarm and looked down at Rossley's body. "I didn't know if he had any more bullets left, and I couldn't let him take another shot at you, Marshal."

Longarm bent and picked up the derringer Rossley had dropped. "As it happens, this is a one-shot gun. But you didn't know that, Constable, and I'll testify to that if I ever need to. Besides, it's been a while since I've run across a skunk who deserved killing more than Rossley did." Longarm turned a puzzled frown toward the Mountie. "How'd you get here? I figured you were still back in Bear Paw."

For the first time, he noticed how breathless Ryerson was as the constable gestured toward the rear of the train and said, "Handcar. I started after you as soon as I found out what had happened."

"You mean you pumped a handcar all the way from Bear Paw? Why didn't you just ride your horse?"

"I thought the handcar might make better time once I got it going. Besides, my horse was tired, and I didn't want to risk injuring him."

Longarm just shook his head. "Are all you Mounties such go-getters?"

"We're trained to do our jobs to the best of our abilities. Just like you, Marshal."

Longarm couldn't argue with that. He said, "Come on. Let's open up those boxcars. I got a hunch there are some gals in there who are more than ready to breathe some fresh air again."

Chapter 20

As they approached the first of the closed-up boxcars, Longarm remembered that somebody in there had shot at him through the roof. He said to Ryerson, "Cover that door, Constable. There's an armed guard in there."

Ryerson nodded and leveled his revolver at the boxcar's sliding door. "Open up in there!" he called. "In the name of the Crown, throw down your weapons and open up! This is Constable John Ryerson of the North West Mounted Police!"

For a moment there was no response from inside the car. Then a vaguely familiar voice shouted, "Don't shoot, Constable! I surrender!"

"Open the door," Ryerson ordered again.

Longarm heard the bolts on the inside of the door being thrown back. A moment later, with a squeal of hinges, the door rolled aside. A stocky figure appeared in the opening, arms up and hands empty. Longarm snapped a lucifer to life with his thumbnail, and in the glare of the sulfur match he recognized the beard-stubbled face of Frederick Drummond.

"Well, well," Longarm said with a grin. "So you were in on Rossley's scheme too, were you, Drummond?"

"It was all his idea," Frederick said hastily. "Rossley was the one who said the Mounties were going to run off all the whores, and how we ought to get some women and put them to work for us, and he's the one who sent Chamberlain and McDermott down into the States to find the women."

The words tumbled out of Frederick's mouth, as if he couldn't implicate Rossley fast enough. He had no way of knowing that Rossley was already dead, thought Longarm, so he was trying to make himself look as innocent as possible. Of course, he was probably telling the truth about Rossley being the originator of the plan.

"To kidnap the women, you mean," Ryerson said.

Frederick Drummond shook his head emphatically. "No, sir. I didn't know anything about that until they brought the women back. I thought they were just going to hire some regular whores."

Longarm nodded toward the boxcar. "Are they in there? Are they all right?"

"Sure, sure, they're all right," Frederick blubbered. "Nobody hurt 'em. We just kept them tied up and gagged so they'd be quiet. Nobody even . . . well, tried 'em out, if you know what I mean, eh? Rossley gave strict orders about that."

Ryerson motioned with the barrel of his pistol and ordered, "Climb down from there. Is there a guard in the other boxcar?"

"Yeah, but I'll tell him to go ahead and surrender, like *I* did," Frederick said as he clambered down from the boxcar. "He's not gonna want to die for Rossley and McDermott any more than I do."

"That'd be a waste, all right," drawled Longarm, "considering that Rossley and McDermott are already dead."

Frederick Drummond just gaped at him.

Ryerson took Drummond over to the other boxcar while Longarm went to the door of the one that was already

174

open. Moving a little awkwardly because of the bullet graze on his leg, he climbed up into the car. A small oil lamp burned on a table next to a bunk in the middle of the car, no doubt where the guards slept. The rest of the space was divided by partitions into six compartments, three in the front half of the boxcar, three in the rear. They reminded Longarm a little of horse stalls, only there were human beings in these compartments, not horses. Young women, to be precise. Each compartment had a door, and when Longarm swung them open, terrified eyes peered up at him from the narrow bunk within. Those bunks were the only furnishings. Small barred openings in the floor provided air. These were almost as bad as prison cells, Longarm thought in horror and disgust. For the women, they had been prison cells.

Longarm stepped into one of the compartments and went over to the bunk. The woman lying on it, who wore only a thin shift, had a gag over her mouth. Her hands and feet were tied, and her body was lashed down on the bunk. She blinked rapidly, probably from a combination of fear and being unaccustomed to much light. To ease her mind, Longarm said, "Don't worry, ma'am. I know you don't really know what's going on, but I'm a deputy United States marshal." Carefully, he untied the gag and then pushed thick red hair away from her face. "You'd be Miss Clarissa Ralston, I reckon?"

She nodded and said haltingly, "Th-that's right. You said . . . you said you're a marshal?"

"Yes, ma'am. We got a Mounted Policeman here too. You'll be free in a few minutes, and so will these other gals."

Clarissa Ralston, who had come to Montana Territory to spread the Gospel to the Indians, closed her eyes and said fervently, "Thank God, thank God." She opened her eyes again and looked up at Longarm as he took a clasp knife from his pocket and began to saw at the ropes holding her to the bunk. "I never gave up hope that we would be rescued, Marshal, but sometimes it . . . it was hard not to."

"Hope's a funny thing, ma'am," said Longarm. "It's fragile as a spiderweb sometimes, but mostly it's the strongest thing we got to hold on to."

By the time he had freed all six women in the boxcar, Clarissa Ralston had already climbed out. She helped the others down. All of them were stiff and sore from their captivity.

Longarm took Ryerson's gun and kept Frederick Drummond and the other guard covered while the constable climbed into the second boxcar to release the women being held there. While Ryerson was doing that, Longarm said to Drummond, "Did your brother know about all this?"

Drummond shook his head. "No, Clive and I weren't that close, never have been. It got even worse once that spitfire of a daughter started working with him. All he knew was that I was working on a plan to bring in some young, fresh whores. I had let that slip one day while we were talking. But don't try to make him part of this, Marshal, because he wasn't."

"Well, I appreciate you telling the truth, old son." Longarm was satisfied with Frederick's answer. He figured that when he had brought up the subject of young prostitutes with Clive Drummond, the saloon owner had thought of his brother's comment and had intended to send Longarm to talk to Frederick. Clive might have thought that sending customers to Frederick would be construed as a peace overture. More than likely, Clive hadn't known that his brother was no more than a minor partner in Rossley's scheme.

That pretty much cleared up all the questions, thought Longarm. . . .

Until Constable Ryerson hopped down from the second boxcar and said, "There are only five women in here, Marshal. Weren't we looking for twelve in all?"

Longarm stiffened. Six and five made eleven.

One of those missing women from Montana Territory . . . was still missing.

Emily Sue Preston was the one unaccounted for. Longarm questioned all the women as they gathered in one of the passenger cars and the train backed toward Bear Paw. Ryerson had Frederick Drummond and the other prisoner under guard in the second passenger car. Dr. Davis checked over the women and pronounced them in reasonably good health considering the ordeal they had been through. Although it embarrassed most of them to a certain extent, they all confirmed that they had not been molested while they were held prisoner. Rossley had kept them as fresh as possible, especially the virgins, knowing they would bring higher prices that way.

But none of them remembered seeing Emily Sue Preston, daughter of Mrs. Agatha Preston, the seamstress at Fort Benton. They had all been together in the closed-up wagon after Chamberlain and McDermott grabbed them, and there had never been more than eleven of them.

So where was Emily Sue, and what had happened to her?

Longarm didn't have any answer for that, and it was clear that he wouldn't find one here in Canada. Back in Bear Paw, he said his good-byes to Queenie and Rufus, Claude Renoir and Jeremy Stubbs. Queenie wouldn't have to worry anymore about her uncle taking the saloon away from her. For one thing, Frederick would be going to prison for his part in the scheme, and for another, Queenie's father had regained consciousness and was starting to make a slow but steady recovery.

"I'll sure miss you, Custis," Queenie said to him before he rode out. "Having you around made things even livelier than usual."

Longarm grinned. "You can probably use some peace and quiet then."

"As long as things doesn't settle down too much. I don't

177

think they will. Bear Paw's going to be a town with the bark still on it for a long time."

"I reckon you're right about that," Longarm agreed. "But you and Rufus can handle things."

"Rufus is a pretty good fellow, isn't he?" Queenie said, a thoughtful expression on her pretty face.

"That he is," Longarm said, glad that her thoughts were going in that direction.

The last person he bade farewell to was Constable John Ryerson. "If you ever get down to the States again, look me up," Longarm told him.

Ryerson nodded. "You can rest assured I'll do that very thing, Marshal. I enjoyed working with you. If you ever decide that you want to move to Canada, I'm sure a place for you could be found in the North West Mounted Police."

Longarm just grinned and shook his head. "I reckon I'm too much of a maverick for that. Anyway," he added with a wink, "the Mounties already got one redcoat who don't mind bending the rules a mite when he has to."

Telegrams had been flying between Canada and the United States. In a few days, the women who had been rescued from the boxcars would be escorted to the border by Ryerson and several other Mounted Policemen who were on their way to Bear Paw, including Inspector Sam Steele, who was in charge of cleaning up the railhead. They would be met there by a detachment of cavalry from Fort Assinniboine and taken back to their homes.

Despite his satisfaction with the way the case had worked out, the mystery of Emily Sue Preston's disappearance still nagged at Longarm as he rode south. He was still chewing it over in his mind when he came to the little roadhouse and tavern run by the man named Ashford, where several days earlier he had met the old mountain man Dooley McCarren and his squaw Little Fawn. Longarm almost passed the place by, but then he decided to rein in and stop long enough to say hello to Ashford, who had been a friendly enough sort of gent.

The first person Longarm saw when he came in was Little Fawn. He thought about backing out again, but he couldn't move too fast with his leg still stiff from that bullet graze. Anyway, she had already seen him and came toward him eagerly. "Custis Parker!" she exclaimed, surprising him a little that she remembered his name. She had heard it only once that other day. This was also the first time he had heard her voice. She hadn't said anything to him before Dooley came in, only wiggled around on his lap, and she had whispered to the old mountain man.

She threw her arms around him, pressing her lush body against him. "It is good to see you, Custis Parker," she said. "You are the most handsome man Little Fawn has ever seen."

"Well, uh, that's mighty kind of you, ma'am," Longarm said as he tried to disengage himself from her passionate embrace. "You don't want to be carrying on like this, though. Ol' Dooley might come in and start waving that hogleg of his around again."

Little Fawn gave an unladylike snort. "Dooley does not care about Little Fawn anymore. He cares only for the little yellow-haired girl."

Longarm frowned and asked, "What little yellow-haired girl?"

"The one he brought to live with him. The one he hides in his lodge."

Longarm felt something go through him. "When was this?" he asked. "When did he bring the girl?"

Little Fawn shrugged, which made her impressive breasts move against Longarm's chest. "When the moon was last full."

Longarm did some fast figuring. Three, three-and-a-half weeks earlier, he decided. Not long after Emily Sue Preston vanished from Fort Benton.

Well, son of a bitch, he thought.

He put his hands on Little Fawn's shoulders and moved her back a step. She looked disappointed and a little angry. "Listen to me, Little Fawn," Longarm said. "Are Dooley and the girl at Dooley's lodge now?"

Little Fawn pouted. "Why should Little Fawn tell you?"

"Because it's important," Longarm insisted.

She shrugged. "They are there. Girl told Little Fawn to get out. Dooley should have punished her, but he did not."

"Take me there," Longarm said.

She moved closer to him again and insinuated her pelvis against his. "Take me here," she said.

"Maybe later."

"You promise."

Longarm gritted his teeth. "All right, I promise. Just take me to Dooley's lodge."

Five minutes later, with Little Fawn riding behind Longarm and rubbing her breasts all over his back as she held him around the waist, they came up to a large, buffalo-hide lodge. Dooley had lived among the Indians for so long that he didn't know any other way to live. The old man must have heard Longarm's horse, because he stepped out of the lodge and quickly pulled the entrance flap closed behind him.

"Well, howdy," he said as he looked up at Longarm. "Didn't expect to ever see you again, mister."

"This meeting's a surprise to me too," said Longarm. Behind him, Little Fawn slid down off the horse. Longarm went on. "Where is she, Dooley?"

"Little Fawn?" Dooley asked with a frown. "Why, she's right there. Hell, she was on your horse, you oughtta know where she is."

"I'm talking about Emily Sue."

The shot went home. Longarm saw the flash of fear in Dooley's eyes before the old-timer could control it. "I don't know what you're talkin' about."

"Sure you do," Longarm grated. "I'm talking about the gal you stole from her mama down in Fort Benton—"

A young blond woman in a buckskin dress suddenly burst out of the lodge. "Leave him alone!" she cried. "He didn't steal me! I asked him to come get me! I *begged* him to come get me!"

Longarm looked down at Emily Sue Preston and asked, "Why in the world would you do that?"

Tears ran down her cheeks as she said, "Because he's my father, and I love him. And because I couldn't stand to live with my mother anymore."

Longarm took a deep breath. That wasn't the answer he'd been expecting. He looked at Dooley, who had slipped an arm around the upset girl's shoulders. "Is that true?"

The old mountain man nodded. "Aye, it's true, though I don't see what business any of this is of yours, mister."

"Because I'm a deputy U.S. marshal," Longarm said flatly, "and Emily Sue is one of the women I was sent up here to find. Somebody was kidnapping young women down in Montana Territory."

Dooley gulped, and Emily Sue went pale. "Pa didn't kidnap me," she said. "I swear it!"

"You see, Marshal, Agatha and me never did get along," Dooley said. "She couldn't abide a wanderin' man, and I was never the sort to sit at home. Always had to be off adventurin'. So she kicked me out, or I up and left, or somewhere in between those two. Anyway, I was gone, but I missed my little gal here. I sent the money I got for my pelts to Agatha, for her to put away for Emily Sue, and sometimes I got letters, but it weren't the same as seein' her for myself. When she wrote to me and said she wanted to leave . . . well, I reckon I knowed it was wrong, but she said she was gonna run away from Agatha whether I came for her or not, and I sure as hell didn't want Emily Sue goin' out in the world on her own. There's plenty o' bad things can happen to a pretty young gal on her own."

Longarm thought about the McKenzie girls and all the other young women who had ended up as Rossley's prisoners, and he had to nod in agreement. "I reckon you're right about that."

"So I went and got her and brung her back here." Dooley glanced at Little Fawn. "I know her and Little Fawn don't get along too well, and I wish things was better, but all I can do is the best I can, ain't that right?" Plaintively, he added, "You ain't gonna take her back to Agatha, are you? Why, hell, that ol' bat hates me. Won't even use my name no more, wouldn't let Emily Sue use it neither."

Longarm tugged at his earlobe as he frowned in thought. He didn't know if Dooley had actually broken the law, and besides, Longarm didn't have any jurisdiction up here in Canada, especially now that the case that had brought him here was over.

But was it really over? As far as Emily Sue's mother and the folks down at Fort Benton were concerned, the girl was still missing.

"All right," he said as he came to a decision. "I'm not going to take Emily Sue back."

Dooley closed his eyes in relief. "Thank you, Marshal," he said. "I surely do thank you."

"I'm not taking her back," Longarm said, "because you are."

"What!" Dooley exclaimed.

"I won't go!" Emily Sue chimed in.

"Yeah, you will, or I'll ride back up to the railhead and talk to the Mounties about this, see what they want to do about it."

"I don't want to go back and live with Ma!" Emily Sue wailed.

"I ain't saying you have to," Longarm told her. "But you got to tell her where you are and who you're with. You may not believe it, gal, but she's hurting because you're gone and she don't know what happened to you. She's hurting bad."

Emily Sue sniffed. "I don't believe it. She never cared about anybody but herself."

"That's where you're wrong." And a spoiled little girl to boot, Longarm thought, but he kept that to himself. "She cares about you, and the three of you got to work this out where everybody's satisfied."

" 'Tain't possible, not where Agatha's concerned," Dooley declared.

"Well, you'll at least try, and that's by order of the United States Justice Department, represented by yours truly. Understand?"

Dooley and Emily Sue both sighed. "I reckon so," the old-timer said. "We'll start first thing in the morning."

"I'll spend the night at Ashford's and go with you, just to make sure you don't decide to take off for the mountains or some such foolishness. And if you run off between now and tomorrow morning, I got an amigo in the Mounted Police who'll help me track you down."

"All right, I said we was goin', didn't I?"

"Just be sure you do." Longarm started to turn his horse away.

Little Fawn reached up to grab his arm and stop him. "Take Little Fawn with you, Custis Parker." When he hesitated, she said, "You promised."

Longarm thought about it, and then held a hand down to her and took his foot out of the stirrup. She smiled, grabbed hold, and swung up behind him.

He had always been a man of his word, Longarm thought with a grin as he sent the horse trotting back toward the roadhouse.

Watch for

**LONGARM AND
KILGORE'S REVENGE**

the 324ᵗʰ novel in the exciting LONGARM
series from Jove

Coming in November!

LONGARM

**Explore the exciting Old West with one
of the men who made it wild!**

**AVAILABLE WHEREVER BOOKS ARE SOLD OR AT
PENGUIN.COM**

(Ad # B112)

J. R. ROBERTS
THE GUNSMITH